ag

Key Principles in History 2

AFTER THE DEATH OF THE GOAT GOD

A Novel

by

Fergal Stapleton

AD1639

Published by Grey Tiger Books

First Edition

Illustrations by Denese Morden
Cover illustration by Audrey Reynolds

ISBN : 978-0-9564419-2-8

Job 39: Knowest thou the time when the wild goats of the rock bring forth?

ONE

In the morning after the smoke had cleared, Agatha van Bosvelt's lifeless body was found in a ditch at the edge of the Biesbosch on the outskirts of the City, and Backer and Meer were down there with her spoiling the sombre mood. They were supposed to be clearing up the mess while ÓDouwe sniffed among the trees, but the heavy rain was slowing progress to a crawl. Backer, with only his nose visible under his antique liripipe, was shoving the head around with a stick, watching how the dirt ran off the skin in rivulets. The hair twined around the face and under the ragged wound, and when he rolled the head in the opposite direction, the hair unravelled and fell free again.

Meer, suspicious of Backer's more thoughtful experiments, tore himself away from his appreciation of the naked body, lolloped over and started making comic faces at the head. 'Look, she's still got one eye open.' And so with a groan Backer bent over, took up the head and jiggled it near his groin.

ÓDouwe quietened them with a grunt.

Backer turned to his master. 'Werkendammers. Or Gorinchem scum, sir.'

'Scum,' echoed Meer.

'Yes, thank you.' The rain was making ÓDouwe's coat heavy and ran off his hat in a thick stream whenever he turned his head down, which he had to do to study the ground. Here were the cold remains of a bonfire, some animal tracks, human footprints too, many of which had no doubt been made by his own men – all of it melting under the force of the rain. No sign of the girl's clothes.

'Alright, get her on the pallet.'

Backer tossed the head towards the rest of the body where on impact with the wet ground it threw up a coronet of liquid mud.

'Carefully!'

The mare shied from this glimpse of hell, but her bonds held her fast to the cart as the men wrestled the corpse towards her, all the while complaining at each other.

'Don't fuck about.' ÓDouwe untied the reins to his own horse. 'I'll be back soon. I want to look at her closely.'

They grinned stupidly.

Ignoring them, he mounted and set off down the waterlogged plain towards the main body of the wood. His men, settling into the cart after a brief scrum for the driving seat, carried the corpse in the other direction toward the Virgin City.

○

The squatters' camp consisted of a couple of dozen hovels cobbled together from scraps of sail or plank. Their architects were universally understood to be the lowest grade of human – hanging-material every one of them – foreign, idolatrous, poor, lazy, thieving, dirty, unwanted. They congregated here at the withered edge of civilisation, alternately feasting on stolen meat and starving, while having their numbers regularly thinned by stringent doses of the Law. But they refused to disappear entirely: they were tenacious, they were sly, and above all,

they were abundant breeders.

As ÓDouwe picked his way between heaps of filth, his gloved hand resting lightly on his sword, heads poked out of hatchways and gaps. An emaciated – sheep? – tried to scurry away, but was yanked back comically when it reached the end of its rope. Bony mutts of every permutation pricked up their ears. One came forward to assess the strength of the enemy and decided to advance no further.

Mrs Janse was already outside standing to attention, her thin body bundled in rags soaking up the rain. He swung around her in a slow wide arc letting his horse judge how close it wanted to get to her. Like the dogs, her children turned their hungry stares on him too.

A black shape flitted from behind the hovel and charged into the wood. All human eyes followed it. ÓDouwe spurred his horse to a canter and, leaning close to its neck to avoid the low branches, zigzagged through the trees. The shape was agile and dodged at crazy angles in and out of the thick undergrowth, but the horse was agile too, and faster. As he closed on the fleeing figure, ÓDouwe recognised him. 'Lennep! Get back here! Lennep! I know it's you!'

Lennep stopped running, turned around and came back panting, getting his excuses in straight away. 'Sir, I was just checking on them. I thought I heard something.'

'Shut up.' ÓDouwe turned his horse, used its neck to nudge Lennep back in the direction of the camp. 'What were your orders? Watch them from a distance.'

'I was cold. It started raining.'

'I don't want to hear it. You were with the woman, weren't you?'

'I kept an eye on them. They're all still here, sir.'

'How do you know? They could have killed you and left anyway. Should have.'

Back at the camp, ÓDouwe pulled up his mare in front of Mrs Janse and leaned forward to let the rainwater run off his hat. 'How much he pay you, then?'

'Four stuivers,' she said.

'Christ.'

'Should I make her give it back, sir?' asked Lennep.

ÓDouwe dismounted. 'Get the boy.'

'We're hated for bringing you,' said Mrs Janse, watching Lennep slope around her.

'Well then, what difference does it make?' ÓDouwe squinted up at the far ridge of trees, and followed the crescent of the outer edge of the wood back down as far as he could before the trunks directly in front of him broke the view. 'Don't suppose you saw the fire up there.'

'Saw no fire, sir.'

Lennep dragged the boy forward and deposited him in front of his master. ÓDouwe put his hand under the boy's chin. He was rigid, shivering, thin, sullen, dumb. He hardly blinked as the raindrops pattered on his cheeks and collected on his eyelashes, but his eyes swivelled away as ÓDouwe tried to look into them. 'You can do that much, you can do more. What did you see up there? Paul, isn't it? Who did you see up there? Did you know her? Who was with the girl? Were you watching them at their work, is that it?'

'I told you he hasn't talked since,' said the mother.

One corpse more or less, one dead dog more or less… ÓDouwe considered the quality of the boy's silence, indicating radical novelty in his experience in the woods or, alternatively, a sensitivity to violence unusual in his breed. But a rank swamp like this? Could it produce a philosopher, a poet, a human? All the strands binding this to that having snapped, what indeed was there to say? First the murder, this way, that way, and then again the murder, and by the way the murder, and coming right up, the murder…

'How old is he?' ÓDouwe asked, not looking at the boy's mother.

'Twelve.'

'Then you're a man, and there's no need for this. I know what happened was bad, very bad. It made me quiet too. Even my men—' He guided the boy by his elbow away from his mother towards a tree-stump and eased him down into the iridescent puddle that had collected there. There was a wrong sort of lightness to him, like a falling object. 'I'm not saying you did it. Of course you didn't. Though there's blood under your nails, and on your clothes too.' He held up the boy's small, unresisting hands, letting the rain wash out the dark stains. 'You can't very well deny it, even with your silence. I know you've had enough already, but try and see it from my point of view. You needn't look at me if you prefer, but you must listen. It's important, not for me but for you, and for your Mother and your brothers and sisters, and everyone else here. Now, this blood comes from that girl. We'll leave aside the question of how it got there. But let's say you saw who did it, and that it was even someone here, a friend of your Mother's, and so it's natural that you prefer not to say anything about it. But it's also natural that you should. I understand your problem and I'd like to fix it for you, but you mustn't indulge this sudden passion for silence to the detriment of your family, must you? Here, you can scratch his name in the mud with this stick.' ÓDouwe called over to the mother, 'He can write, can't he?'

'Some.'

'Or I can— Paul, I can have the men parade in front of you and you can point out the guilty one.' The boy shivered on his stump. 'Your Mother tells me no-one likes you anymore because of me. Well, as things progress, you might become even less popular, and you can hardly blame me for it later.'

He paused to show he was still willing to give the boy his chance.

‘Or you saw nothing, yes, I can accept that possibility. You saw only the girl, already dead, and you came back here and haunted your Mother with that white face of yours and everyone’s blood curdled with horror. And here I am now adding to your misery. But you can see that I must if you refuse to tell me.’

The boy stayed as he was, unmoved.

ÓDouwe brushed off the leaves caught in the burr of his damp clothes, went to his mare, laid a hand on her nose and remained in that attitude, facing away from all of them, staring at his horse’s neck. All eyes except Paul’s followed him. Then with a few brisk actions, he settled his sword, arranged the reins, climbed into the saddle and urged the mare on.

Lennep, hoping for orders, put himself in front of his master. But ÓDouwe was already cantering away before he shouted back at him to stay behind and get himself killed or do what he pleased.

○

ÓDouwe raised the corner of the sheet to expose Agatha’s feet. The toes were translucent, small, pink, hardly used. He pulled the sheet off and bundled it away, remembering, despite himself, the assessments of his men. Even lying inertly, she possessed elegance. Can a corpse be said to be unmannered? He placed his thumbs on the highest points of her hip-bone and caressed lightly, just once or twice, and tenderly observed the gentle upward pattern of hair decorating the soft mound below her belly. Then, fastidiously, his face tense with rueful tact, he separated her legs and examined the generative apparatus (choosing that term in this moment) for evidence of congress and found no bruising or damage there.

With some difficulty, he turned her over. Again, no sign of rape, no sign of attack. He let his eye linger a moment, for respite merely, on the

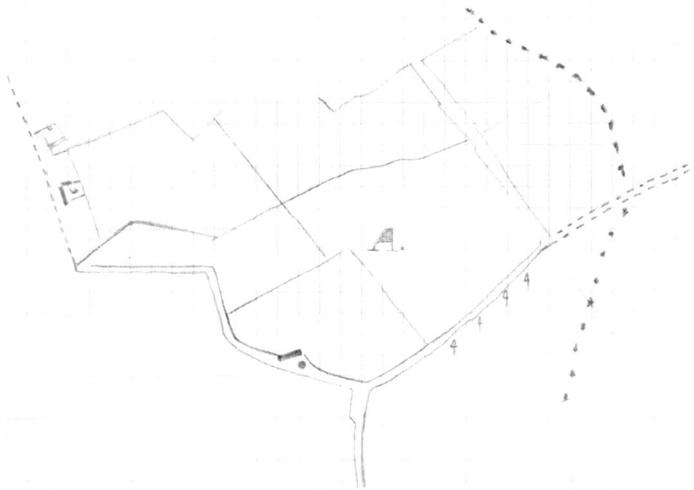
A.

fine soft pale hairs that lined the cleft of her buttocks.

He rolled her onto her back once more and lifted up one of her hands. How small and strange it was, like a delicate crab skin that, once shed, provides starker evidence of the miracle of life because of its useless beauty. The nails on it were unbroken. Nothing was caught under them, no hair or flesh or blood that he could see, and it was the same with the other hand. No sign, then, of defence.

He moved up to the neck. Bone and flesh glistened in the dark hole. The skin was ragged and stretched. Some of the tendons and muscles were likewise stretched and protruding from the gash. It was as if the head had been torn with great force from the body, but there were no other tears or marks of severe distress on the surrounding area as he had seen on criminals who had been racked, for example.

When he was done, he arranged her head as best he could above the shoulders and covered her with the sheet, carefully tucking it under her chin. Given her condition, dressing her seemed too absurd a prospect, but with the pathos of a tender act performed far too late, he placed a cap on her crown.

Her open eye, which ÓDouwe had not been able to close, continued to stare at the ceiling as if it could penetrate all the way through the plaster, wood, tiles, clouds and sky to whatever mysteries may with serene aloofness inhabit the stratosphere.

○

They're scattering in every direction! A massacre! A genocide! What fun! (But necessary.)

Under the slanting rain, ÓDouwe's force had become restive at the prospect of action, and relieved the tension with expressions of bloodlust for 'scum', 'vermin', and, according to Backer, moved to a rare prolixity, 'sloppy sewer-shit fit for sluicing.'

What followed was real enough, though to those involved it may well have unfolded within one or other of the various divisions of the dreamlike: tidal drags of inevitability, thick-aired halt and restart, rainbow-edged fervour… For some it proved a broiling nightmare, for others a conscienceless spree.

ÓDouwe's own nightmare was afterwards complicated by a wide-awake professional anxiety: how to objectively judge – given the fresh gaping wound in his head – to what extent and in which direction progress had actually been made.

'Alright, alright, keep it down,' ÓDouwe hissed, trying vainly to preserve a quiet privacy in which to pick over his puzzle: surely there were better ways to accomplish the stated aims of this expedition (discover physical evidence, make arrests) than swooping like vultures on a carcass. A share of resentment had established itself in several places in the equation. He felt the reach of his power compromised by unworthy forces: the craven appetites of soldiers; the vulnerability of his branch of officialdom to capricious fluctuations in personnel and rearrangements of rank; the beggars themselves exciting the instinct of the hunt in citizens, soldiery and State officials alike.

But another element seeped into the puzzle, its blood perhaps, independent of the main organs, flowing wilfully, eluding any prolonged examination of its properties, which otherwise might be summarised as the blending of two profound irritations: the life of the girl, the silence of the boy.

'And keep those dogs quiet,' ÓDouwe added. 'Arrests only. No killing. And don't forget the girl's clothes if they're here.'

This was received for the most part with blank looks.

He turned his face up to the heavy mass of cloud to let the fat drops do him some cleansing good. 'They're all dressed in rags. Anything fine may well be hers.' He leant over to his deputy, Roel ten Brink. 'Someone better stay with the wagon.'

The man ten Brink chose dismounted, went over to the barred wagon and slumped disconsolately against one of its massive wheels.

The rest formed a loose arc and cantered forward.

When the hunters sighted the hovels, their joy was unbounded. They whooped and galloped ahead, churning up the soggy ground, wildly swinging their cudgels. When they reached their target, they overran it, trampling everything under hoof. Panic spread through the camp. The inhabitants ran in every direction, slipping in the mud, yelling at each other, grabbing their children, tripping over their own dogs who had caught the contagion of terror, and falling under the weight of the confused horses and the flailing weapons. Ten Brink divided his energy between leading the attack and trying to rein in these excesses.

Some of the hunters' hounds broke free and dashed into the mêlée, and the others were let go to follow them. The hounds' preferred targets were the famished dogs now so maddened with fear that they turned with despairing fury on their attackers. 'The dogs!' ÓDouwe yelled, 'kill the dogs!' and some of his men drew swords and slashed at the beasts, making little distinction between their own and the others, which enraged the houndskeepers who rushed in to protect their own. Some understood ÓDouwe's order to include the people as well.

Others were meanwhile tearing the rags from the women, imagining in their zeal that they had found the rich girl's finery.

ÓDouwe's horse dropped to its knees and he toppled over her neck. Again he turned his face to the now blood red sky. He retrieved his sword, brandished it at no-one in particular, bared his teeth and tried to hear himself bellowing orders which no-one took any notice of. The general din concentrated itself into a single note, that of the pit, he thought, where the hate is, the slowed down convulsions, the stretched mouths, the gore, the chaos, the wretched stupidity.

Meantime, Lennep was running here and there, not knowing whom to attack or defend, so that he found himself pirouetting ineffectually in a deepening puddle at the eye of the storm. Backer and Meer broke off what they were doing – kicking a man while he was down – in order to protect Lennep and also to mock him.

When the din finally quietened, three dozen of the vagrants lay dead, many of the women were half naked, and there was plenty of other damage besides. Certainly, it had been a bad day for dogs.

While the others bundled the captives into the wagon, and ten Brink supervised an orderly search for the missing clothes, ÓDouwe bandaged his mare's leg. When he was done, he went in search of Paul whom he found cowering with his mother and her other surviving children behind their hovel. Fearing the approach of the final blow, they gaped in terror at the spectacle of that mask of blood.

'What do you say now?' he asked the boy.

○

Everything of Mrs van Bosvelt's house seemed bigger than it needed to be: the gate, the path, the steps, the door, the windows, the sign identifying it as that of the Lions Triumphant – all ample, carved, coloured and patterned beyond reasonable need. Woven within the broad decorative effects on any given surface were smaller schemes of design revealing an odd underpinning of disharmony, as if this were secretly a monument to straining chaos.

Maria, the handmaid, her eyes pink from constant crying, had Mr ÓDouwe wait while she went to speak to her mistress. It took him a moment to get his bearings. At first, he had mistaken her for a regent rustling towards him in her deep coal-black satins, but as soon as she had spoken, he had realised his mistake: she too was an ample decoration.

The vestibule in which she left him gave panoptic glimpses of the various rooms on this floor. Servants paced past doorways, through arches, along corridors, and up and down staircases, briefly encountering each other in silence.

After a few minutes, Maria came back. 'Sir, she says she won't see you today.'

'What are you talking about? Haven't you told her?'

'No sir, I only said it was about Agatha. I told her who you were.'

'Tell her again. No, wait, I'll come with you.'

Mrs van Bosvelt was in the room, but gave the impression that she had not yet arrived in the room, or at least was not fully aware of having done so. The space she drifted within was punctuated by gargantuan furniture, glinting ornament, curiously liveried staff, and a host of gilded, unappealing pictures: rows of solemn progenitors above, and below them, judging by the costumes, the current dynasty. And over there, all around the bloated alien chimney-piece looking more like a shrine to fire than it ought, a handful of pictures of a small child ÓDouwe presumed to be Agatha when she was much younger.

Almost uniquely in this city of pictures, ÓDouwe himself possessed no such item. And yet here in the Virgin City, there were fifty different kinds, and a thousand examples of each kind: food, fields, whores, the old, the young, the past – why never any of the future (unless you counted those colourful views of the Last Judgement, which he didn't, they being curiously of no sort of time at all)? What would such a thing look like? He squinted at the ones of Agatha, but got no further than imagining the young girl as a middle-aged woman.

Once the mistress's eyes caught him, they instantly gave no sign of letting go. Had her people told her something after all? He addressed her. 'Madam, I am Mr ÓDouwe of the Superintendent Bailiff's office. Unfortunately, I have tragic news concerning your daughter.'

'What are you saying? Who are you?' Her voice was narrow and unpleasant, incongruously pitched for spite and caprice. The sudden impression was of a self-devouring bird (appearing sketchily in his imagination as an Egyptian deity of anger). This was replaced impetuously – with a hint of occult trickery – by an impression of a repulsive, tyrannous insect whose regurgitations had painstakingly constructed this mound around her. She and her surroundings supplied the complementary halves of an acutely angular nightmare or a horribly tangled cautionary tale. And this creature was to be understood as the mother of the other creature? The contrast, infinitely stark, provided in itself an extra dimension to the nightmare.

'I am Mr Ollamh ÓDouwe,' he repeated, partly to affirm as in a prayer a fundamental credo threatened with sabotage.

'What? Where are you from?'

'From the Superintendent Bailiff, Madam. I am gravely sorry to have to tell you that your daughter was found dead in the Biesbosch this morning.'

'I can't see you today. You'll have to make an appointment.'

'Madam, I'm sorry.'

'We'll see how sorry. I shall speak to your superior. I fear for your employment at the, at the Ministry.'

'Madam, it's true,' Maria whispered, and quickly put her hand to her face.

Mrs van Bosvelt stared at her servant with vigorous contempt. 'Maria, bring Agatha to me this instant. This instant!'

'Your maid has viewed the body and confirmed that it is that of your daughter,' said ÓDouwe. 'I'm very sorry. There's no doubt about it. I've arranged to have the body brought here, of course.'

‘Who is this person? Maria, why have you brought him here? This is an unspeakable outrage. Show him out immediately and then come and see me.’

‘Madam, I’m sorry,’ ÓDouwe repeated.

Maria wavered at the door. Mrs van Bosvelt rose from her seat and went to one of the windows. There she stayed with her back to them all, moving her head this way and that as if she might be following the carefree flight of a bird in the sky.

○

Available categories of death are manifold, as are the available categories of response to it. This current collision of the two might have given rich material to the connoisseur, but for the duty – new to ÓDouwe, having never before encountered murder amongst the regents – of delivering the news whilst cushioning the blow.

He imagined that the most radically traumatic examples of death – the family wipeout, the foreign massacre – harbouring as they do the possibility of elemental significance, could be borne like fate, like an important block of destiny. Then again, the anguish might be of such perfection as to excite a surprise counterattack: the withheld reaction, the stilled response. Blood could be frozen, memory stabilised into areas of reduced visceral agony – all the standard disciplines of the maniac. Or there was always the option of quenching the fury in fresh blood: other deaths could be added to the toll to blur and assuage.

But having to open oneself to unwanted sympathies…

When the coffin was brought in and laid on its trestles, ÓDouwe discreetly adjusted the position of the head.

After a time Mrs van Bosvelt crept forward and looked into the bloodless face of her daughter with its eye aimed at the ceiling. She stayed in that attitude for a long while. 'This is no good at all,' she said finally. 'We'll have to get a better coffin. Maria, find her best clothes.' She reached in to stroke her daughter's matted hair. The head rolled out of its place. Trying to nudge it back only made things worse. It settled at an unnatural angle and the sheet fell away from the neck. Mrs van Bosvelt drew a breath, reached in, took her daughter's head in both hands and held it up in front of her.

'No!' ÓDouwe put his hand out.

The mother looked into the daughter's open eye which seemed to be looking back with a remote kind of compassion.

ÓDouwe was struck by an illusion of two decapitations, with the mother's ruff like a plate on which her own head was displayed.

'I told you to be careful, didn't I?' Mrs van Bosvelt's tone was not tender. 'I've told you a hundred times, and yet you disobey me. Now look at you…' She shook the head.

Precedents existed too of course for the perfectly crazy response – hurling oneself into the grave after the coffin being a common example, or any failure to recognise death on its own terms. But here was a too perverse combination of reproach, regret and spectral unreality.

ÓDouwe gathered himself, approached, eased the head from the old woman's grip, replaced it in the coffin and covered it with the sheet.

Mrs van Bosvelt went to her chair and sat there quite still with a little expectant look on her face.

○

Outside the house at the sign of Saint Luke Gilding a Lily, ten Brink made his report to his master concerning the Night Patrol who the night before last saw nothing of any importance, mainly because they were not patrolling but drinking. The Watchmen, on the other hand, had been at

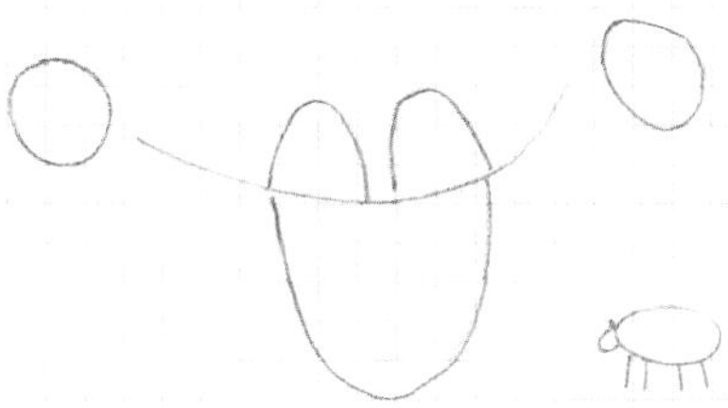

their posts on the ramparts, but said they too saw nothing, and it was ten Brink's considered opinion that this was because they had debauched themselves at the kermis and then slept soundly in the hours between the bells.

ÓDouwe acknowledged these items of unsurprising news with a brief nod before knocking on the door. He brushed the sheen of moisture from his shoulders while he waited. The painting master Gerrit van Oelst himself responded to the summons. Tall, thin and pale, he had the air of a guest given the awkward task of admitting strangers to someone else's house. 'Yes?' he said looking from one to the other as if seeking clues to some deeper mystery than their superficial identities.

ÓDouwe had him lead them into the classroom where the painting students worked. Van Oelst hunched awkwardly between his two visitors as if trying to blend better with his surroundings. During his timid repetition of the introductions and the policemen's stated aim for the visit, the five young students found they had time to fully absorb the view. Mr ÓDouwe proved a disappointment to their youthful taste for typical appearances, expressing none of the expected vividness of a high-ranking police officer, but his deputy seemed more like it, dripping a satisfying quotient of sour, slow-eyed menace.

The painting master's own deputy, Judith Craebeckx, whom they had also come to interview, remained alone, so van Oelst told them, in the back studio – staring out of the window, as it happened, at the rain impacting on the bobbing heads of the flowers in their little garden.

As Mr ÓDouwe made his way towards the door to her retreat, with Gerrit at his heel, one of the pupils, rogue male Cornelis ter Gouw, following his habit, rose to the challenge and emitted what he considered a comical noise which the other boys tittered at nervously.

Ten Brink remained behind to speak to the boys and quickly discovered that they had nothing important to say to him. They knew of no friends of Agatha's, except perhaps Miss Craebeckx. Having rapidly exhausted that aspect of her life, they went on to show how well they had recovered from the news of her death by telling happy stories of her ineptitudes, competing with each other to salvage ever more hilarious details from their memories of her – godawful Pekelharingese most of it. Once, for example, she tripped on the stairs and slid upside down on her back on the wet picture she had been holding. Another time, instead of answering a question, she accidentally farted. When she did manage to say something, her face would burn with shame and she would get all her words mixed up, which when added to her lisp and her stutter, rendered her incomprehensible and marvellously amusing. In the midst of all this gaiety, someone imitated Cornelis's earlier comic exhalation, but he himself remained unusually quiet, absorbed in private regrets – or presentiments. He stole yet another quick look at ten Brink, but the policeman maintained a blank mask. The funny noise meanwhile sparked a riot of copies fuelling more mirth. Some of the boys were moved to improvise a bout of mimicry of their victim's awkward ways: her trippings and fallings, her bumpings-into and butter-fingerings, her lispings, boo-hooings and st-st-stammerings.

Ten Brink, marooned at the eye of this fresh storm, kept his nerve. A little rise of anger stirred to life his own inner pictures of boys having their fingers removed – briskly, with a sharp knife ('there there, all over, here just wrap this around the stump') or their teeth broken, just the one each, with an expertly aimed jab of the knuckle; or their heads shaved and…

Perhaps because they must inevitably succumb to Cornelis's mood, or because ten Brink insatiably absorbed all the fun out of their game, they too fell quiet, and ten Brink was left with the dismal impression of Agatha as a mouse at the mercy of a pack of weasels.

In the back room, ÓDouwe was squinting at Judith's absurdly tiny silhouette and he turned to Gerrit to see if he wasn't making a stupid mistake. She was a miniature, a doll, misplaced too far into the foreground. But he was assured it was her alright, the jewel, the treasure, the one everyone made such a fuss about, but just now she looked like someone who had been hit with a hammer. Experience of pain, memory of pain, what it means, what it says about the future: more pain promised later… They get a look about them. The muscles in the face fail – their job is over, it would seem. The rest sinks under its own weight. Even a light-as-air creature such as Judith was visibly losing a war with gravity.

'My sympathy…' he said, and automatically left a space for any reaction to his accent, but he had said it too softly, which got more of her attention than he had expected. He adjusted himself under her crazily tranquil pale blue gaze. What could she be thinking right now? – about himself, he meant. Was she forming an opinion? Was she even really seeing him? He moved laterally an inch or so. She seemed to notice.

And now she seemed to be asking him for his name. Instead of a squeak to go with her diminished size, her voice was deep, rich, smooth, almost funny because of it.

'Did I not say?' He rearranged himself as he laid out his title before her, including for reasons just beyond his ken, his name in its entirety – an offering perhaps, or a plea, meantime showing her how the scar on the bridge of his nose caught the light, showing the shoulders, the famous hands, the knuckles.

'And what do you want, Assistant Superintendent Bailiff Ollamh Paidraighzoon ÓDouwe?' He found the precision of her recall shocking under the circumstances. Perhaps silence or spools of words would do equally well as diversions from grief. Or if challenge was intended, the triviality of it disturbed. He told her he wanted to ask questions. She nodded and glanced around as if they might come at her in shadowy forms from the corners of the room, but that was the extent of her co-operation. She seemed not to fathom their meaning when he posed them to her: When? Then. Where? There. Or she simply didn't know the answers, or she thought them beside the point, or she forgot to listen, imagining subtler, more harmonious priorities. Or the failure was at the base level of the category itself: What's a question? What's an answer? And of course van Oelst kept interfering, hovering, answering for her, dithering around her, getting in the way, blocking the bloody view. And ÓDouwe couldn't kick him away with her watching.

In any case, when the outcome had become clear to them all, she simply got up to leave, a decision produced not entirely from her own will, but still half remembering some snatches of etiquette, a nod, a smile, a bow, a wave. He saw how she quickly closed her lips over her crowded teeth – a little act of vanity whose power must have momentarily superseded that of grief.

ÓDouwe stayed behind with van Oelst, gave himself leave to take in the man, the buffoon, the spoiler of pleasures. What qualifies such a one to paint pictures? He took in those pictures lining the walls and set on easels. 'These all yours?' he asked, stopping him from following Miss Craebeckx into the classroom. The painter avoided his eyes, began shifting, touching things as if they were someone else's. 'I see you like flesh,' ÓDouwe said, waving a finger at various nymphs. One picture was covered by a heavy cloth. He hooked it up and peeked. 'Oh! You like Judith's flesh.' He snatched the cloth away. There was her minuscule body, small breasts, delicate bony hips. She was taking her weight on her elbows. Her arms were crossed near the wrists, her porcelain knuckles showing through the skin. 'She's got wings?'

'I thought of combining the Sphinx with the Roman augur of doom.' Gerrit dithered around the picture, trying to hide it with his lanky body, trying to pretend he wasn't hiding it.

‘Did you?’

‘This line here…’ He convulsed towards the one between Judith’s joined legs. ‘It flows exactly according to the line of the Nile, which, look, you can see on the map behind her. The Nile is itself a deity, in the pagan… the myths before Christ…’

‘Oh yes. So here,’ ÓDouwe pointed to Judith’s shadowy sex, actually tapped lightly on the surface of the painting, ‘is its source. Is this what pictures are really all about, then? Lust. I mean if they’re not of trees or regents.’

‘I don’t know…’

‘Don’t you? I’m surprised.’ It was possible the painter was telling the truth. Pictures may have been mysterious to their makers also. ÓDouwe let the thought dwindle, not wanting to dissipate energies in byways too occult, preferring to return to the example at hand. ‘Judith Craebeckx,’ He elaborated the clicks in her name, ‘with no clothes on.’

Ten Brink came in and shrugged at his master. That was the sum of his report on the boys. He joined ÓDouwe at the picture of Judith which van Oelst was trying to cover up again. He held back the cloth with his large, gloved hand, staying quiet for a bit before letting the cloth fall. ‘Shall I take the boy now?’

‘Not in front of her.’

‘What boy?’ van Oelst asked, animating himself again. ‘Which one? Take him where?’

They ignored him. ÓDouwe had become interested in another picture, this one unfinished, of a man on a horse. ‘He looks familiar.’

‘That’s Mr Harmen Flinck.’

‘Flinck? Really?’ He raised his eyebrows at his deputy.

‘His Father is… ah, yes, The Hon. Willem Flinck, your very own Superintendent Bailiff,’ van Oelst said.

‘And what was he to Agatha?’ ÓDouwe asked.

'To Agatha? Nothing. He sits in here, same time every Friday afternoon.'

'For the whole time? He comes through the front, doesn't he? Past the class. Are you or Miss Craebeckx always in there every moment of the day? Of course not. You don't happen to know where he lives?'

Ten Brink spoke quietly into ÓDouwe's ear: 'Spends his evenings at Mrs Bleckker's.'

'Why do I not know this already?' He gave his deputy a searching look then turned to a small animal carcass stretched on a table and prodded it. Ten Brink assumed by this movement that the question put to him didn't require an immediate answer.

ÓDouwe stepped in very near to Gerrit, leaving half an arm's length of gap between them, radiating heat at him, making him stop fidgeting and pay attention. 'Who do you think tore the girl's pretty head off?' he said. Ten Brink brushed past Gerrit to have a prod at the small carcass himself. 'Come on,' ÓDouwe went on, 'you must have some idea about her pretty head. I have the matter of a murdered girl in the woods whose head has been removed, and I have yet to discover the culprit whose special pleasure it is to do such a thing. Did you fuck her?'

Ten Brink seeing this interrogation was likely to produce no more useful result, and anticipating his master's next likely action, turned from the carcass, bent down and put his eye to the keyhole of the classroom door. Van Oelst frowned at the proximity of his hindquarters. 'No.'

'No, I don't think you fucked her when she was dead and then cut her head off, or cut her head off first and then fucked her which would have been even more unusual, because you are not unusual, are you?'

'I didn't,' said Gerrit. Another little convulsive movement coursed through him.

'Oh? Too young? Not young enough?'

'For the love of Christ!'

Ten Brink spoke into the pause. 'She's just left.'

ÓDouwe straightened himself.

Once again, all three men stood at the head of the class, presenting a curiously fluid and uncertain arrangement, subtly different from before. In particular, the bailiff was glaring into the room with an eerie tense concentration. (The other two were in their contrasting ways aware of a duty to wait and see what he would do next.) He was considering the pupil ter Gouw: a schoolboy wishing to expand the range of his supremacy ought to learn to consider the consequences of failure as well as success, this after all being a school... During the pause that produced this professional conclusion, ÓDouwe's expression had begun to resemble that of an iconic saint poised in the equilibrium between conflicting mysteries, and because of this became the sole focus of the boys' soundless attention.

'Go on then,' he said finally to his deputy.

Ten Brink instantly stirred himself and moved among the pupils, laid the weight of his hand on Cornelis's forearm, measured the force of the resistance he found there, swung round and struck him under the chin, immediately drawing from the boy soft tears and far-reaching regrets. The other boys quickly understood with varying degrees of satisfaction that they were being treated to a subtle moral entertainment. Ten Brink pulled Cornelis by his arm. He cried out to Mr van Oelst, but his master was suddenly busy with his own dense emotions. Ten Brink led the boy by his hair out of the house to the canal's edge where a barge was parked. The barge-boy hunched on his horse in the rain barely seemed to notice the two of them and ignored Cornelis's wasted plaint as ten Brink dragged him aboard and threw him through a hatchway into the bottom of the boat.

It was cold and wet down there. Cornelis righted himself and peered into the shape-filled shadows searching for the source of the sniggering he could hear. The source was Backer and Meer and they lurched out of those shadows and started kicking him, laughing all the while, pushing each other about as well. Cornelis, grunting and yelping, rolled around the filthy water in the bottom of the tub trying to avoid their blows.

The barge began to move.

Using a slow pace, Mr ÓDouwe came down into the barge and stood to one side leaning against the hull seemingly lost again in his own thoughts, used to all this. 'Go on,' Backer was saying to Meer. Meer showed his green teeth, flailed his fist at Cornelis's blotched face and recoiled with a squeal to inspect his injured hand. 'Look, I'm bleeding,' he said, showing where his knuckle had caught on the boy's teeth. 'Let me try again.' ÓDouwe waited for this second experimental blow before telling them they could stop for now, and they slunk away elbowing each other through the narrow doorway.

ÓDouwe waited for the boy to heave himself up into a squatting position. He was breathing hard, spitting blood, shivering and holding his ribs. 'I've been having a think about you,' ÓDouwe said, 'your future. This could be it here with those two. What do you reckon to that?'

'I don't know, sir,' Cornelis wailed. 'Why did they hurt me? I've done nothing.'

ÓDouwe tutted but otherwise did not reply.

After a time, Cornelis tried again, stifling his anguish. 'Please sir, where are we going?'

ÓDouwe considered the question. 'Where? Towards your future. So, you want to be a painter?'

Cornelis dared not answer, failing to see any connection between that situation and this.

'It's alright, you can answer,' said ÓDouwe extending an open hand in the boy's direction.

'A painter? Not really,' Cornelis wheezed, 'but it's not so hard. My Father told me I had to study something.'

'Your Father? You want to bring your Father into this? Who is he?'

'You may know him. He's an Almoner.'

'Is that a good thing? Making himself a bore to honest drinkers. Does he know about you?'

'No.'

'What do you want to be when you grow up?' Again Cornelis hesitated. 'Go on,' ÓDouwe encouraged him, 'I want to know.'

'A policeman?'

ÓDouwe laughed out loud. 'Yes, but that would be up to me, not you, wouldn't it?'

'Yes.' Cornelis adjusted his position, tried to stand up.

'Stay where you are,' said ÓDouwe firmly, showing the limits of any indulgence. Cornelis slipped back into his puddle. 'Now suppose you tell me all about Miss Agatha van Bosvelt whom you saw for several hours every working day for the best part of three months.'

'Agatha? She was stupid.'

'I heard she was very bright. What else?'

'Teacher's puppy.'

'Mr van Oelst's?'

'Miss Craebeckx's'

'Hmm. When I saw her, I noticed she was very soft. How soft did you find that she was?'

'Eh? Very.'

'Yes, very. And how many times, more or less, did you test this softness in this puppy?'

Cornelis looked up, genuinely interested. 'I never touched her. I've been going to whores for more than a year. My Father pays.'

'Ah, your Father again. Is he so thoroughly steeped in illegality?'

'I mean I use his money. He doesn't know.'

'I'm becoming keenly interested in your Father. Fathers seem to be a theme recently. And what about Mr van Oelst. Was Agatha treated in any special way by him?'

'He left her alone mostly.'

'Who else?'

'Mr John Norvell, Miss Craebeckx's father's secretary. He's always around.'

'Always around Agatha?'

'Always around Miss Craebeckx.'

'Ah, and what about the others? The people that come in to do business with Mr van Oelst. Mr Flinck, for example.'

'We like him. He's funny. Even Agatha liked him, I think. He was nice to her.'

'Was he? And what about Miss Craebeckx and you? What about that?'

'Nothing. She's alright.'

'You're very big for your age, aren't you? Do you think you're very big for your age?' Cornelis looked at the wet floor. 'Miss Craebeckx, I noticed,' said ÓDouwe, 'is very small. I almost burst out laughing when I saw her. Really quite comical. Very, very funny. And yet she pisses all over you from up on high.'

Cornelis chewed the inside of his mouth.

'No, really. All over you. You're positively drenched in her piss. I can smell it from here. It's almost as if you like it. Do the whores you see… now how can I put this delicately? Oh, don't look so sad, Cornelis, I'm only having a bit of fun. I work so hard and there's so little time to relax and enjoy myself. And now this.' He inhaled deeply. 'Cornelis, you go ahead and be the policeman for a minute, like you said. Take on my burden.'

The boy watched carefully from under his eyebrows.

'Who do you think did it?'

Cornelis shrugged.

'Don't go disappointing me now. You gave me such fun earlier when you said you wanted to be a policeman. So now's your chance. Unless… no! You weren't laughing at the police by saying that. Laughing at *them*?' ÓDouwe indicated his men on the other side of the door. 'Come on now, try again.'

'It wasn't me,' Cornelis said, quickly wiping a fresh tear that had begun to flow from his nose towards the corner of his mouth.

'But you said yourself that she was exquisitely soft exactly like a dog that you begged to piss on you but she refused because you didn't know how to beg properly and wanted to be shown how by your daddy, didn't you?'

'Yes.'

'Yes.'

ÓDouwe leaned back. Cornelis, still clutching his sides, saw that if the interview was coming to an end, it were better he himself added nothing more – provoked nothing more. He was also acutely aware of the fulcrum on which poised his immediate future: either the worst was over or it was yet to come. The darkness, his fear, the opacity of the policeman's face all prevented him from knowing which was the more likely. Other sounds filtered into the dank space: the horse's hooves; the occasional encouragements of the barge-boy; the water lapping on the other side of the hull. These were supplanted by harsher noises indicating that the barge was finally being moored.

'Ah, good, we're here.' ÓDouwe turned away and climbed up the steps. Meer came padding down the same steps and grabbed Cornelis by his ear and led him up to the light where the others were waiting at the canal kerb. Cornelis had been half expecting the stone walls of the gatehouse prison, but there were only ordinary houses here. His captors assembled loosely to one side of him, bowed slightly in the grey drizzle, not paying him much attention. He thought of running, but felt his trembling legs wouldn't carry him very far. The barge-boy had dismounted and was feeding a medlar to his horse and stroking its neck as if everything in the world was as it should be. Cornelis understood that his ordeal was in its final stage and dared to begin a favourable reshaping of the last half hour's experience.

'I'm tired of you,' ÓDouwe said and Meer ran at Cornelis who wailed, flinched and instantly revised his feelings of the previous few moments. But Meer simply shoved him into the stinking canal. 'Why don't you swim home?' said ÓDouwe.

○

The end of the world is on its way. Yes, yes. The important questions are: date and time, who's in, who's out. But John Norvell could hardly concentrate on these questions because of the hearty feast that Agatha van Bosvelt would shortly be supplying to the Harpies and their agents, the glittery-eyed feeders that creep over the Earth or flap out of its hot cracks to gorge on the soft flesh falling off the bone, the melting tendons, the peeling fibres, the skin turning to phlegm, the face collapsing into its own mucus and the churning maws awaiting it…

'What?' He was drawn from his reverie by the escalating volume of the debate.

On the other side of the front door, a pop-eyed eavesdropper and his deputy were meanwhile attempting to commit to memory a stream of novel information produced by this debate concerning human history past and future: the several Seals, the Empire of the Whore, the chimera, the horses, the riders of the horses, the visitations of the various Messiahs false and true, the terrible Dragon, the Muhamedist, the blood, the silenced oracles, the apostolic progeny, the Time of Careful Provision, the Corruption and the Reformation, the mystical deaths, the great numbers and the small numbers, the shutting up of the Beast, the palm-bearers, the twelve hundred and sixty years, the many trumpets, the thousand years, the general agonies, the Last Day, the extinguishings of light, the Final Judgement, the twenty-five years – from now? – the wormwood and the mortifer – twenty-five years? – and the Little Book wherein the destiny of the Church is writ.

And additionally a great deal of matter about the various writers of the Bible were gone over in a spirit of high animation, and indeed the feasibility of the story of the first family itself, and the parts of Revelation already fulfilled and those yet to be, and how human thought is in itself a reliable source of revelation because God would not allow error in a sound mind, and how faith and prayer might prove the decisive factors in the purity of the reception of such revelations, and how the books of Moses tell only of the emergence and development of the Jews and not of all Mankind, and that the Gentiles preceded the Jews on Earth, and that an original True Religion preceding that of the Torah might be discerned from the clues inherent in Pagan beliefs, and that the planet Venus had recently passed across the face of the Sun.

Was such density of detail, compacting under its own weight, produced in order to sufficiently relate a tale of time, illusive substance, coming to a stop? Or would that be specifically Biblical time, a substitute species of the stuff, by turns illuminated and blotted by friars? Or were they looking merely at a bloated tale of death, one isolated instance of which, repeated over and over again, might finally transform into forked lightning, brassy notes, rent azure?

ÓDouwe had not intended to loiter so long outside Norvell's door exciting the curiosity of passers-by. But he could hardly forego this opportunity to receive uncensored a dispute hinting at bounteous harvests of control.

Persuaded by a sudden increase in the downpour, he banged on the door at last. John and his guests exchanged looks of disquiet. The callers strode in without the slightest show of tact and immediately began scrutinising the inhabitants. 'Name? Address?'

John Norvell introduced himself first. Ten Brink, noticing his withered arm being the only part of him not included in his nervous motions, got in closer and prodded it, but it still showed no sign of life. For ÓDouwe, hope surfaced, however weakly, that amongst this menagerie there might be found cause for virgin sacrifice.

He pulled up a chair while his deputy brushed past the men and disappeared deeper into the house. 'Any of you chaps acquainted with an Agatha van Bosvelt?'

Nobody spoke.

'I'm a bleeding policeman. You have to answer my questions.'

They shook their heads quickly, all except John, who nodded.

'I already know about you,' he said to him and turned back to the others. 'I see. So, I'll just sit here and you gentlemen carry on as normal. No? Private matters? Secret matters? Quite understandable.'

Still they kept quiet.

'So what are you all doing here, then? You for instance, what do you do for a living?'

'We are all philosophers,' boomed Erlach, a German who was... ÓDouwe took a second to gauge possible threat, and concluded... *tall.* 'Specialists. I for example am a student of the great Peyrère.'

ÓDouwe stared at him.

'We were talking about light,' added Burn, a small, dark Scot. ÓDouwe transferred the stare to him. 'What makes it, what it's made of,' was

Burn's supplementary comment.

'Not the Divine species, but that which derives from the sun,' added ben Bezalel, a Jew, older than the rest.

ÓDouwe began filling his pipe. 'Everything, everything…' He thought for a moment. 'What's a clever word for it? Coagulates? Conjoins?' He made circles with his hands to conjure his elusive word.

'Converges?' John suggested.

'Conspires. Yes, Divine Will, human intelligence, whatever else there may be of that kind. And here I am. And here you are.' He puffed smoke at them and gazed into the glowing bowl. 'Yes, tell me. Light.'

'Um…' said the Frenchman Fleurant, 'I was explaining that the denser the object through which light passes, the quicker it does so.'

ÓDouwe made no response, no movement. He seemed entranced, as an animal on its first encounter with a human. When he saw the man was unwilling to say more, he snapped back to life. 'And what did you all have to say to that?'

Everyone murmured, nodded, searched for the next thing to say.

'That's all? After—' he took in the empty plates, the open books scattered on the table, '—all this time? No, you're being too modest. There was more. Come on, I'm not as delicate as you might think.'

'If you must know,' said the German Peyrèriste, 'we were also discussing the possibility of unifying all knowledge within a single master discipline. It's a subject with many possibilities, many avenues. As men who value learning—'

'You know,' ÓDouwe interrupted him and turned to John, 'we already have a great superabundance of Johns and Jans and Johanneses. For instance, you want to guess what my third name is? Or his Father's name?' He pointed roughly in the direction of ten Brink whose footsteps could now and then be heard elsewhere. 'And we seem to be importing them as well, and from where? Wales, is it?'

'England,' said John.

'Well, yes, there is a difference. And despite the excess, we welcome you here. Don't we?' ÓDouwe lighted on Fleurant. 'Don't stop now. Keep the flow going. These things get nowhere if it's all fits and starts.'

Ten Brink reappeared at ÓDouwe's shoulder and whispered into his ear.

The Cartesian struggled on. 'I, in that spirit, to, to unify um, revealed revelation, religion, and the discoveries of natural philosophy…'

'Really?'

'And also the conversion of the Jews which…'

'Ah.' ÓDouwe twisted around to look curiously at ben Bezalel.

'…Which…'

'Yes,' ÓDouwe inhaled through his pipe, controlling the intake with two fingers playing lightly over the bowl, and nodded several times.

'…Not that…'

'No,' said ÓDouwe, 'not at all.'

Troost, a fat man, seemingly the only true native amongst them, took up the slack: 'And how we have, I and others, I mean, have written to the effect indeed that the States, these States are ideal for the, for the, for any learned or progressive project.'

'Progressive,' ÓDouwe repeated flatly.

'Yes, because the, of the great, the very great, very liberal, within the auspices of the Faith…'

ÓDouwe stretched forward, groaning as he did so, tapped the remains of the burnt tobacco onto a plate, and increased the severity of the blows until the speaking stopped. When silence was fully established, he stood up. His deputy was waiting to lead him out of the room. 'Yes, you'd better come too,' ÓDouwe said to John.

When the three of them reached what seemed to be the topmost room in the house, ten Brink indicated a ladder behind a screen. ÓDouwe climbed it and found himself in a large square turret.

'What's the matter with your arm?' ten Brink asked John, prodding him again.

'I was born with it.'

They emerged into the turret. In front of one of its many windows was a telescope fixed on a tripod. ÓDouwe put his eye to it. 'Very cosy. You can see who comes and goes from here, can't you.'

'I'm interested in astronomy.'

'Aha, and who's that in the window, I wonder?'

'Looks like the painter's house,' ten Brink said.

ÓDouwe was watching a miniature image of Judith resting her forehead on the glass, almost as if she were leaning against the lens an inch from his eye. 'Your friends don't know about you, do they? I bet Judith doesn't. What, I wonder, are you up to? Up here watching the world, like a twitchy-nosed crippled little godlet. And downstairs, you've got your clandestine gatherings.'

'I wouldn't say clandestine,' said John.

'I would. Not for you the open drinkhouse or the public highway to discuss your business. Rather, whispering amongst yourselves, with no-one around to twist your meanings and cause all sorts of undeserved trouble.'

'Well…' John nervously watched ten Brink poke around in his things. 'There's no real mystery. I worked at Law before coming to Craebeckx.'

'No you didn't. You copied for a lawyer, and not a very good one. Look what he's done for your present master, Mr Craebeckx. Father of Judith. Whom you annoy with your sweaty presence several times a week.'

Ten Brink was holding one of John's many notebooks.

'Do you have girls up here? Seems like a good place to have girls,' said ÓDouwe.

'No, I don't.'

'Men?'

'Sometimes,' John said, then saw what he meant. 'No, I'm not a criminal!'

'What, then? Who are those men downstairs, really?'

'They're really scholars, philosophers. Nothing more.'

'Not liars, then? Or conspirators, madmen, or fantasists? Or plotters and idolaters?' ÓDouwe turned to his officer. 'A scholar is a man who writes down what other people say. And a philosopher is another name for a God-botherer.'

Ten Brink nodded at his lesson.

'And the twenty-five years?' ÓDouwe continued to John.

'Ah.'

'Ah, indeed.'

'Well, it's not so important. It's just that certain interpretations of Revelations… from the Romans to now, a sequence of events… in Revelations… that shows that that's about the duration… before the first tumults… the final thousand years…'

'Of?'

'Everything. Us…'

'The United Provinces, then.'

'No, I mean, within the greater scheme…'

'Not real, then. Made up.'

'Well, there's been some disagreement… It's only a…'

Ten Brink meanwhile radiated odium at John, who fearing himself about to be more tangibly assaulted, found his voice become increasingly shaky and quiet, until he gave up the struggle to talk altogether.

ÓDouwe reapplied his eye to the apparatus. 'So from here, you could see Agatha van Bosvelt going to school, going to her friend's house. You might have seen her with someone the other night. Did you?'

John withdrew quickly from the threat of another lapse into bleak reverie. 'No.'

'What about other times? Who have you seen her with?'

'No-one at all. Judith only. Or her maid. That's all.'

'Do you find that people confide in you quite a lot, John?'

'I suppose…'

Ten Brink had settled himself in the corner and was using the fading daylight to illuminate John's writings.

'It's almost as if we were colleagues exchanging ideas about a difficult case before throwing our hands up and uncorking the port,' ÓDouwe continued. 'You have that quality about you. I feel comfortable in your company. You're the kind of man I could use. Have you ever thought of a career in the police?'

'No, I hadn't…'

'You sit up here in this secret room watching everyone come and go. You know what they're up to while they're in the dark about you. And what's this? Notes on their movements?'

He was addressing his officer again who said in a monotone, 'Some.'

'It isn't really…' began John.

'And the rest? There's enough of it. What is it all?'

'Various things,' John said, 'Natural philosophy, medicine, theology, painting, music, astronomy, that sort of thing.'

Again ÓDouwe consulted his man for confirmation.

'Some,' the officer repeated, and handed over the notebook.

'Ah, and all in French, I see.' He flicked through the pages. 'And German, Spanish… and Swiss is it? And John here is English,' he said to ten Brink.

'Fucking foreigners,' Ten Brink replied, picking up another notebook.

'Yes, there's not much nonsense to Roel. No frills. Born of this soil, and he knows what's what. But I must take the sophisticated view. I'm not allowed the luxury of simple truths expressed with earthy vigour and then quickly forgotten. My responsibilities cannot be summed up in patriotic epithets. Do you follow me?'

John's distraught spirits, seeking respite, giddily made some claim on ÓDouwe's frank manner, and even on the foreign unfamiliarity of the face – fellow strangers together, he thought. 'But where are you from, yourself? Ireland, isn't it?'

The policeman remained as he was, as if he were waiting for John to speak, as if he had not spoken. Ten Brink held motionless the page he was turning for a moment, then turned it. ÓDouwe said to ten Brink, 'The English are responsible for most of the trouble in the world. Did you know that?' Then he said to John, 'We'll have to take all this. We'll have to go to the trouble and expense of having it read and translated and summarised. Then someone, perhaps myself, is going to have to interpret its significance, if it contains any, and make some sort of plan about it. With regard to any action. With regard to you.'

'Once you're satisfied it's harmless, could I have it returned intact? It's very dear to me.'

'Could we?' ÓDouwe asked his officer.

Ten Brink shrugged.

'Now, I don't know who is supposed to cover this expense. My superiors have me in a very awkward position. I'll have to do the work, but they won't be keen to pay.' ÓDouwe stared at John with such intensity that John felt obliged to scour his mind for ÓDouwe's meaning.

'Money!' John exclaimed at last, and the policeman laughed and nodded. 'How much? You realise I'm not rich.'

ÓDouwe looked about the room as if appraising the truth of the statement and explained reasonably that the man he would have to hire would be exactly like John: a secretary with some education. Or perhaps he would have to find several men, each representing a fragment of the knowledge which John had recorded.

Ten Brink was meanwhile going around the room with a large bag tossing all the notebooks into it.

'A florijn a week,' John said rather desperately.

'Hmm, I would have thought a florijn a day,' replied ÓDouwe.

'But I simply can't afford that.'

'I know, I know, but you can get your friends downstairs to chip in, can't you? That's their charge for lying to my face. And know that they're getting off very lightly. It's a shame I can't literally use you. Not this time. You can see why.'

Ten Brink unfastened the telescope from its tripod and threw it in the bag with the other things.

○

The sign of the Black and Gold Fireship indeed vividly conjured an elemental scene on a whipping ocean, as might seem apt for a whoreshop. The Mistress of the house, Madam Bleckker, like the house itself, of indeterminate antiquity, and bearing many scars of uncertain provenance, led ÓDouwe into her inner salon. He braced himself. This region of the underworld, decorated in rare shades of lemon, royal purple and flesh, an unruly combination, summoned for him queasy visions of baby animals engaged needlessly in precocious carnalities. 'Harmen Flinck here?'

Mrs Bleckker flicked her one good eye at ÓDouwe like a lizard. 'I'm afraid I don't know the names of my guests, Mr ÓDouwe.'

'You know mine.'

She managed to express a crude contrition with her dead eye. 'Indeed. Perhaps a description of the gentleman?'

He peered into his memory at the man in the picture. 'Tall, thin, groomed moustache, twenty-five, rich, full of himself… Pale eyebrows?'

'Indeed.'

'Better if you get him, I think, rather than me.'

Madam Bleckker nodded.

'Did you know the girl that was killed?' asked ÓDouwe.

'The little rich girl? Judith brought her once or twice, but she barely spoke to me.'

'Brought her *here*?'

'Yes. Sat her right there where you are. Judith used some of my girls for her pictures. Strange little animal, Judith's mouse, bigger than its master, if such a thing can be imagined, always following, giving out occasional little squeaks.'

'What was Judith doing with her, do you think?'

'She wanted a pet? Money? Her Mother ordered it? I don't know. I'll go and get him.'

With Harmen Willemsz. Flinck using a practised casual asymmetricality, keeping his eyebrows raised and his lips pouted, trying to hide the fact that he had been drinking all afternoon, ÓDouwe found himself reflecting on the differences between men and pictures of men. Flinck expressed his indignation at ÓDouwe's refusal to stand up in a series of small movements which travelled like a slow pulse of light down his body, through his fingers all the way to the finely embroidered gloves which began to flap and twist at his thigh.

Mrs Bleckker hovered behind him, rolling her good eye at each of them in turn. In place of her other eye the thin film of scar tissue seemed horribly watchful in its own way.

'Kind of you to interrupt your afternoon's business.' ÓDouwe waited for his words to penetrate the coils of fog.

Harmen said nothing for the present, merely worked rather too visibly on his posture. He was handsome in a pinched way, pale under the eyes and rouged at the cheeks, with additional colour supplied by the exercise of his hobbies. ÓDouwe was thinking of him as someone who applied himself to his debauches with the air of a man with no talent to avoid, no life's work to defer, unlike the better sort of drinkers and whorers who actively and perhaps courageously embraced defeat. He was that type of man with no point to him, no character, nothing of interest to himself or anyone else. A rarity of that kind might well prove dangerous to a virgin.

Harmen gave up the series of little battles with his equilibrium, leaned against the door and exhaled alcoholic fumes. 'I was told it was vitally important. Has something happened? Is my Father alright?'

'Your Father? Your money's alright.'

'What? What, then? Look, I'm quite busy.'

'I'm–quite–busy.' ÓDouwe repeated the words flatly, inspecting them individually. 'You know that girl we found with her head torn from its socket?'

'Yes, yes, very bad business. Everyone is tremendously upset, yes…'

'Well, I was thinking that since you knew her—'

'I didn't know her.'

'Since you knew her through Mr Gerrit van Oelst who is painting a huge picture of you trying not to fall off your horse—'

'Oh.'

'—that you might tell me something that would help me bring to justice the shiftless oaf who did it.'

'Like what?'

'Like who did it.'

'I don't know. I hardly knew the child at all. Alright, yes, I go there.'

'A lot.'

'He's a damned slow painter.'

‘So you’ve had plenty of time to work your charm.’

‘I told you. Look, who are you working for? My Father is already looking into this matter. We’re all very concerned.’ He turned to Mrs Bleckker, but she was careful to show him only her dead eye.

‘Are we?’ said ÓDouwe. ‘Have you not heard of me, Mr Flinck? Am I not famous in your circle?’

‘Forgive me, it was an unfamiliar name.’

‘This is Mr ÓDouwe, sir,’ said Mrs Bleckker. ‘He is a very important policeman.’

‘Thank you Mrs Bleckker,’ said ÓDouwe. ‘May I call if I need anything?’

‘Of course, sir.’ She bowed to them both and closed the door after her without any further sound.

‘ÓDouwe?’ Flinck tried the name out. ‘Where’s that from?’

‘From your Father, Harmen. He has given me all necessary powers to catch this criminal. He tells me he is acquainted with the victim’s family. As are you. He has instructed me to leave no stone unturned. So here I am, turning the stones.’

‘But this is sheer insolence. Allow me to warn you right now, Mr ÓDouwe. A magistracy awaits me. Some other fate may therefore await you.’

‘Yeah, but I don’t give a fuck for you or your rise. Like I said – like your father said – I’ll be disposing of you as I see fit, though you may not me, so kindly cease your noise. Now, does your father know you go around breaking the laws that he spends all his energy trying to enforce for the good of the City? Does he know you undermine his efforts at every turn?’

‘I? But I do no such thing.’

‘You fuck whores. You’re not allowed to. What would he say?’

‘I don’t know.’

'Alright then. Do we have an understanding at last? You sit down and stop acting the arse with me and we might get somewhere.'

Harmen slumped into a sofa and pulled a sullen face.

'Now, here you are in this house as we have already established beyond any doubt. What is in doubt is what you've been up to all this time with that young girl. Have you been charming her out of her tree? I hear tales, you know.'

'Well, I talked to her, yes, but I talk to all of them. It's my way. I like to be friendly.'

'Did she say No to you? I can easily understand a man's feelings under such circumstances. I've seen her too, don't forget – alright she was dead by then, but...'

'I talked to her, that's all. I never touched her. I never suggested touching her. Yes, she was pretty. Yes, I liked to flirt a little. But she was too bloody awkward anyway. You couldn't get three straight words out of her.'

'Harmen, the people above me, the girl's Mother – it's because she's so distraught I suppose – I'm under a great deal of pressure. Even your Father, as I said before. Everyone is worried about it, what damage it could do to the City's reputation. Imagine the complications if it turns out that a *citizen* has committed the crime.'

'Citizen? What about all those bloody foreigners at the kermis? Look, can't you hang some damned villain and have done with it?'

'I've already thought of that, but you see it's not so easy. I still have to tell whoever did it not to do it again.'

'Ha! Very good!' Harmen broke into uneasy laughter. 'Don't do it again you naughty murderer! Ha, ha, ha!'

'Harmen?'

'What?'

'It's not you I have to be careful about. You understand that, don't you? Look, it's my neck either way. I may as well proceed as I see fit, since whatever happens I'm going to get into trouble with someone. Everyone's embarrassed about this thing. It's already dragging on too long, and the longer it drags, the more embarrassed they become, and you know what the result of it all is? They aren't satisfied with the usual answer: some street scum or crazy husband. They want more. They want to go higher. They're convincing themselves of it. You read the papers. You see the trouble I'm in. And they don't see the consequence of it: more trouble.'

'Do people care so much? I don't have a lot of time to read.'

'Harmen, what's a gentleman?'

'A gentleman? Well, it's, let's see. A man with, or a man of wealth, station, property, responsibility. Learning. Of the better sort. Higher than most.'

'Because, you see, I have to view it from all angles. Because I'm in the middle of it. I, alone. You see where I have to go with this. High, yes, but at the same time low.' ÓDouwe made the appropriate mimes with his hand.

○

Judith Craebeckx was wedged tight between the two shrunken, yellow-eyed old men, one – her father – baked (Island-baked) three shades lighter than the other – her father's servant. ÓDouwe had not expected to see her there. He quelled a reflex to reach out to her. Her head was bowed and her shoulders heaved now and then as the servant Culo burbled into her ear just as he had often done in the past when she had been in frequent need of consolation. Meanwhile, Isaac Craebeckx twitched and tutted and listened carefully to Culo's words of comfort so that he could imitate them.

ÓDouwe himself was a larger than usual presence in this compactly partitioned space. He remained standing with his back pressed against the panel and watched the three of them in action. Culo was a curious creature, registered by his employer as a family member in order to avoid the tax on him. Could tell-tale signs of servility nevertheless be detected in him, or indeed native traits of a savage, murderous bent? All he was doing for now was laying with accomplished solicitude one of his gnarled hands on Judith's shoulder.

Craebeckx stretched out his hand too and let his daughter support its weight for a while. 'Well sir? What do you want of us at this very early hour,' he said, 'unannounced as you are, unexpected as you are? We are aggrieved, as you can see.'

The type was instantly recognisable. Men like Craebeckx imagined themselves absent from the picture of the world they perceived, all the while grossly impinging on it, obliterating much of its detail. Judith was such a detail. ÓDouwe addressed the old man. 'Sir, I am painfully aware of the grief on which I intrude, and would rather avoid it altogether. However, I perform the will of the Superintendent Bailiff which is to discover the criminal in this tragic case.'

Craebeckx patted Judith's shoulder heavily once or twice before bringing his hand to rest on the table next to his other one. 'And what will you here, with us?'

'It is the Superintendent Bailiff's will,' ÓDouwe said, preferring to look at the top of Judith's head rather than her father's face, 'that I understand the circumstances of the girl's life so that light may be shone on her death.'

'I fail to understand.'

'Nevertheless, it is the Superintendent Bailiff's will,' – eyes still on Judith – 'that I familiarise myself with all who were connected with Agatha van Bosvelt. Ask questions. Find answers. Discover the truth.

Not explain myself.'

Judith raised her head. The face had sunk further, not only down but back. Features were blurring at the edges of expanding mottled flesh. The pale eyes were sparking with underpowered hostility. She stood up and began to gather the dishes while Culo slid along the bench to make way for her.

ÓDouwe experienced a twinge of regret, but could see no means of keeping her with them.

Craebeckx was meanwhile attempting his own sharp look. 'I am not acquainted with that great family, though my daughter does enjoy the privilege through her daily activities.'

'We have already spoken, Judith and I.'

'Have you?' Craebeckx stared at the side of his daughter's head. 'Well, the Superintendent Bailiff's will must be performed in full. Please proceed.'

As ÓDouwe dragged out a chair and lowered himself into it, Judith crept from the room and they all paused to listen to the sound of her light footfalls on the stairs.

'Where's she going?' Craebeckx demanded of Culo.

'Let her go,' Culo answered, shaking his head.

ÓDouwe stretched out his legs as far as he could in the small space and waited for the tremors to settle. The two old men, unlikely complementary halves, stared out at him. Craebeckx was trying to show authority through a farrago of postures and facial expressions which ÓDouwe didn't want to look at. The servant, on the other hand, was now hardly moving at all, like a breathing mannequin, unwholesomely serene, as if waiting to be re-animated.

'Where you from, Culo?' ÓDouwe said in a strained tone of mild, patient interest.

'Java, sir,' replied the servant.

'Ooh exotic, far away, hot. That where he picked you up, is it?' ÓDouwe nodded in Craebeckx's direction. 'All those years ago?'

'Yes sir.'

'I have to say you don't look like one of them. Human origins are a particular interest of mine, I might tell you.'

'They said my Father was Portingese, sir.'

'Catholic, then. Now, they're the ones that teach you to read so that you *can't* read Scripture, that's right isn't it?'

'I suppose so, sir.'

Craebeckx leaned forward. 'May I know the relevance of all this, Mr ÓDouwe?'

ÓDouwe was finally persuaded to face him. 'And you're one as well, aren't you?'

'We're all Mennonite, praise be to God,' Craebeckx answered, pursing his lips religiously.

'Oh, you are now. But before. Down in the Islands, you were both naughty little Catholics, and when you changed, you didn't even have the sense to change to the right one. Mennonite!' He chuckled.

'Really!' exclaimed old Craebeckx.

'Yes, really. And what else have you been up to? Flower futures? Shouldn't you have known better? The Bankruptcy Court beckons, does it not?'

Stung by this reference to vile taboo, the old man exhaled and slumped.

Disregarding Craebeckx once more, ÓDouwe went on. 'Culo.' he sighed. 'Culo, like the vole that intimately knows its territory. That means *arse* doesn't it? In Spanish, of all things. Should we be having Spanish names, do you think?'

'I'm told it's to do with the English Bottom, sir,' said Culo, 'a humble character in a comedy.'

ÓDouwe was interested, if not disconcerted, by the lack of emphasis the servant placed on the word comedy when he so easily could have done otherwise. 'English?' he said. 'That's hardly any better.'

'Well, it's also short for Immaculado, sir. I was called the short form of my name as a child, so it stuck.'

'And you're not really one of the family here, are you?'

'Legally, yes sir, I'm a Craebeckx.'

'Legally, is it? Culo, let me ask you something. What do you know about a man called Zijss?'

The old men exchanged a yellow-eyed look.

'Came to the old house from time to time. When we had a house. A bad lot. Mr Craebeckx has suffered from his ill doings. As you can see.'

ÓDouwe paused to satisfy himself that invoking the name of Craebeckx's former rogue colleague was more than gratuitous baiting. All leads must be examined. A line of suspicion worth exposing plausibly joined the persons of the *partner* of the *father* of the *teacher* of the murder victim. He flicked a crumb from the table. 'What if we just hung them all? What do you think about that, Culo?'

'Sure would put a stop to a lot of stuff, sir.'

'Sure enough.' Also plausible to a slim degree was that the old retainer harboured a gift of occult power imported from his hot island. Or it could be he was just that type of a person, able to shape himself to the purposes of those around him, such creatures having first placed their own purposes out of the reach of anyone, including themselves. An unknowable quantity, then. ÓDouwe inspected him for a moment in the light of this unknowability. Even the old crab seemed relatively easy with him. ÓDouwe wondered whether he himself might not be responding vicariously to tendernesses extended to Judith, or was in some other wise being smoothed over. 'You know how these things usually end?' he went on. 'Of course you do, an old slave like yourself. The culprits often don't even have the wit to disguise their own guilt.

Even if they don't wait patiently by their victims until we arrest them, all we usually have to do is travel in a spiral out from the corpse and before too long there he is sitting with his head in his hands and a bloodstained knife on the table, or nearby there's three different people ready to repeat the tale he's told them out of pride, remorse or sheer stupidity.'

'But this time it's different, sir.'

'Yes it is. You didn't do it,' ÓDouwe twitched in Craebeckx's direction, 'he didn't do it, nobody did it. Did I do it?'

'Doubt it, sir,' said Culo.

ÓDouwe nodded slowly, and with a fresh inquisitive air he said, 'Do you know what my men are like? Half-wits mostly. Morons, beasts, vegetation. I may as well round *them* up and hang 'em. Then see the crime rate plummet!'

'Yes, sir,' replied Culo obediently, raising his eyebrows and trying to focus on this curiously depressed animal.

Whatever spell the old slave was weaving, ÓDouwe felt himself in danger of succumbing to it. 'So let's see, you tucked your master up in bed—'

But now the door was being urgently rapped. Culo slid out of the room and returned with Lennep running ahead of him. He was out of breath, disarranged, failing once arrived at his destination to say what was on his mind.

'What are you doing here?' demanded ÓDouwe, 'What is it? Don't just stand there with your mouth open.'

Lennep found his voice. 'Mr ten Brink told me to come and get you, sir. He said to come and get you and not leave without you because there's been some mistake.'

'What are you talking about? What did he say exactly?'

'He said come and get you. That's all. Because the girl is back. I saw her myself. Does this mean the investigation is over, sir?'

ÓDouwe stared into Lennep's face for a long moment. 'Alright, let's go.'

TWO

Agatha's ghost, unclothed, with one arm outstretched, walked unsteadily towards its former mother. At each of its uncertain steps, the mother retreated, screaming. 'Madam My Mother, it's me,' the ghost kept saying, 'It's me. Don't you recognise me?' But in vain. The mother was rigid with… spite?

It returned to the maid, Oopjen, and took two or three steps in her direction, but the maid backed away from the horrifying apparition. 'What's the matter Oopjen? You're frightening me. Stop it. Stop it.'

Maria, the other maid, held herself still against the wall in the shadows.

The apparition turned to its mother again whose face expressed a bitter mixture of terror and malice. 'I'm frightened!' it said as it ran at Oopjen and caught her arm before she was able to escape. 'Look at me, look at me! What are you doing?' It began to sob. It held the maid tighter. 'Is it a dream? What's happening?'

Feeling the hard reality of its grip, smelling the familiar odours of the living girl, Oopjen reached out a trembling hand to her face, felt it to be warm, the tears wet, and whispered, 'It's you, it's really you.' And she ran her hand down the face and over the neck which was as whole and unblemished as ever it had been. She then erased the last three days from her mind, as if someone else's thoughts had somehow slipped in amongst her own. 'Here.' She held up a gown for Agatha, obviously not a ghost.

Agatha looked down at herself confused at her nakedness. As she slipped into the gown, she saw the crimson-lined coffin for the first time. 'What's this? What's happened? Who died? Tell me! Please, why won't you tell me?!'

Maria gave herself away with an involuntary movement.

'Maria! What happened? You'll tell me, won't you? Whose coffin is this? Why is it in my room? Am I still in my dream?'

Yes indeed, Maria had heard of this kind of thing, where a person seems to be dead, and is laid out ready for burial and unexpectedly wakes up from what had turned out to be merely a trance. Her mind, too, was able for the present to obliterate the matter of the completely severed head, a symptom from which no-one could possibly recover.

'Why won't you speak, Maria?' Agatha went on, 'I had a bad dream, that's all. Please say something.'

Mrs van Bosvelt found herself unable to bear this perfect nonsense a moment longer. Her face was the grey mask of one who has glimpsed a fragment of hell after having failed to turn away quickly enough. Without another word, she swept past them all out of the room, down the stairs, and out of the house, drawing the door hard behind her.

○

Everyone watched ÓDouwe expectantly as if he were about to reveal the secret behind a clever conjuring trick – except Agatha, who was cramming food into her mouth and washing it down with a large pot of beer and water, some of which dribbled over her chin and was uncharacteristically wiped away on her sleeve.

ÓDouwe meanwhile considered the creature. A block of nausea was slowing down the meanings it was delivering to him. Unused to sifting information with his stomach, he was bound to experience difficulties. A tatter of ancient schooling distracted him: a picture of a Chinese in approximated national costume frowning at his own belly. ÓDouwe's head was clearly out of commission, reeling, staring into space, hiding, peeking.

Of course, he didn't touch her. Not as such. Not as yet. But he knew

it was inevitable that he would because he must, every verification demanding its due.

The Chinese lesson was replaced by one in which Agatha was stripped naked for a repeat performance of his examination of her. But feasibility, relevance… This followed by a yet new shape rising among the ruins: this girl was merely a repetition, another version of Agatha, a better version, removed backwards in time prior to her death, delivering ÓDouwe from the impossible…

Then again, dreams can sometimes be full of colour and plausible incident, seemingly lasting for days. And in those dreams within dreams within dreams, each instance of surfacing into apparent wakefulness, however vivid, always proving paler than the real thing when it eventually comes. Which would this be, then?

Ready to grasp any available aid, he saw that the people around him could offer none. Dream or not, action was demanded – in this case an act of resistance against heavy tides of phantasmagoria. He reached out a hand quickly, perhaps to steady himself, and laid it firmly on Agatha's forearm. He found it to be warm, solid, female, young, alive, present here and now. A doctor couldn't have done better. Or one of those philosophers, asking… asking… how it is we know that we know.

Agatha broke off from her feeding to register the intruding hand. And in that glance – quotidian, dumbly reactive – along with the blood-warmth and give of her flesh, was the information he required just then – that this situation, whatever else it might be, contained a sufficient quotient of normality, at least to the girl, for ÓDouwe to carry on. 'You look like someone who hasn't eaten for a while,' he said, and everyone turned to Agatha to consider this statement for themselves. Agatha nodded. Lennep got in close for a better look.

ÓDouwe let go of the arm and anchored himself discreetly to the edge of the table, for once in his life thankful for Lennep's casual stupidity.

'Girl,' he said, 'do you know these people?'

'All except him, sir.'

'Give her some room, Lennep,' he said with unaccustomed gentleness, which caused Lennep to glance curiously at him. 'And what about me?' ÓDouwe went on to Agatha, 'Do you know me?'

'No, sir.'

'Are you certain? Look at me carefully. Be sure now.'

She obediently focused her eyes on ÓDouwe's face and shook her head.

'Alright, you can finish your meal.' He turned to the others. 'Everyone out.'

Following on behind them all, shutting his eyes tightly, insisting exclusively on the practical, nearly letting slip a groan to go with the effort, coughing instead, he opened his eyes, straightened up and made sure the door stayed ajar. He positioned himself where he could still see Agatha, and began whispering his commands: the coffin to be removed; Lennep to stand sentry at the front door; the maids to take turns at Agatha's side and to never leave her alone; and all to say nothing to anyone outside the house. 'And where's your mistress gone?' he asked them. Nobody knew. He picked out a manservant to go and find her. 'Don't worry,' he said to the frightened man, 'you don't have to talk to her. Just find her and come back and tell me where she is.' The empty coffin made its way back out of Agatha's room borne by two servants. 'The rest of you, clear off.' He stopped Maria with an outstretched finger. 'You can start the vigil.'

He and Maria went back in. Agatha had eaten everything on her plate and emptied her cup. Her upturned face, smooth and blank, a crumb at her lip, sensationally of the world, of which she was blithely unaware. 'Well, Miss Agatha, we had better have a proper talk.'

'Yes, sir.'

‘They may have told you by now, my name is Mr ÓDouwe, and I am the Assistant Superintendent Bailiff which makes me a bit of an important personage in these parts. Do you know what the Assistant Superintendent Bailiff is?’

‘You work for the Magistrate, sir.’

‘Indirectly, yes. My job is to enforce the Law, to catch criminals, to maintain order. And do you know why I’m here in this house at this moment?’

‘No, sir, I don’t. But I know something bad has happened. No-one will tell me, though everyone’s being very nice. I don’t understand. Are you going to tell me?’

‘For the present, it’s important that I don’t tell everyone everything. That’s one of the methods I use to catch criminals. Not that you are one. Don’t be alarmed. You haven’t done a thing wrong. No, but I think you might know of a crime, even if you think you’ve forgotten it. That happens sometimes. Sometimes, in my work, people have to be persuaded to remember important things. And that’s the purpose of this talk we’re having now. Do you understand?’

‘Not really, sir.’

‘Well, just answer my questions simply and honestly to the best of your ability, and don’t worry about a thing. How do you feel? Are you well fed? Well rested?’

‘Yes thank you, sir.’

‘Good. And what day is it today?’

‘Today? It’s… I’m not sure… is it Tuesday?’

‘Quiet!’ he barked at Maria who had opened her mouth. Stung, the maid closed her mouth and looked unhappily into a far corner of the room. ‘And tell me, Agatha,’ he went on, ‘where were you yesterday?’

‘At school. I’m learning to be a painter.’

‘Are you indeed? So yesterday was…?’

'Monday?'

'Are you sure?'

'Not really. I'm a bit confused. I think it was.'

'So it was the first day back at school after the Sabbath.'

'Yes.'

He considered this lapse, which could at a stretch be a general lapse, shared by all. But his own memory of the preceding days was clear and firm, upholstered with a mood of continuity, credibly picked out with incident, sequence, consequence. He stopped himself from consulting Maria for confirmation. 'You know it's really Thursday today.'

'Is it? I must have made a mistake.'

'There are some days to account for. Missing days. Can you account for them?'

'I just made a mistake, that's all,' said Agatha. 'I came home from school. I had my supper with my Mother. I came up here with Maria. We talked for a bit. I went to bed. When I woke up this morning, everyone was behaving very strangely.'

'And I'm told you mentioned a nightmare before,' ÓDouwe said, noting how each new thought animated the girl's features. 'What was it about?'

'I don't know. I can't remember it now. A crowd, a boy, livestock. I don't know. It made no sense. It was just a dream.'

Agatha's relation to boys – Agatha as a discrete figure (dead) in a geometric arrangement (who was where and when?) – had been of interest for a practical reason (find the murderer), now outdated (she's no longer dead). So, under these new conditions, her relation to a boy in a dream might reasonably provide new direction for that interest. 'Did you recognise the boy?'

'No, sir.'

'If you saw him again in real life, do you think you might recognise him?'

'I don't know, sir.' She unfocused her eyes in recognition of some incongruity in the question.

ÓDouwe in turn received a tender ripple from this disturbance. 'Why do you think you were so hungry when you woke up?'

'I don't know, but I was ravenous, wasn't I? I don't think I've ever eaten so much in all my life.'

He let this little enthusiasm subside before asking his next question: 'Why do you think there was a coffin in your bedroom?'

'I don't know. Maybe that's why I had the nightmare.'

'Especially if you'd slept in the coffin.'

'That would be worse.' Agatha glanced over at the spot where the item had rested on its trestles, her malleable features starkly denoting, as in a play, scoured memory, bewilderment. And like an acted character, she played sincerely, outwardly, seeing all but self.

'Everyone tells me you are a very shy young woman. Painfully so. Extremely timid. Barely able to look another person in the eye and speak to him. Is that the case?'

'Yes, I'm very shy, it's true.'

'Is it?' said ÓDouwe, staring into her eyes. 'You don't seem very shy to me. Here we are having this conversation in a perfectly normal way and you don't seem the least bit timid to me. You seem quite unafraid.'

'No, you're right. I feel different.' And to Maria she said, 'He's right. I feel different.'

'And your impediments of speech that everyone has told me about. They don't seem very marked to me.' He turned to Maria. 'Are they improved too?'

Maria was surprised. 'Yes, they are.'

Not that this was entirely new to him. Terrors such as those that had rendered Paul silent might have stimulated comparably extreme, though opposite, changes in the girl. Then again, aggressive timidity can be assuaged through the agency of strong drink. But those doctors of the soul who use that method need long practice to master and manage their prosthetic selves. No, it was thirst merely, the body's requirement for liquid, that urged Agatha to repeatedly up-end her cup into her mouth and refill it from the jug.

The denser convolutions within the puzzle, as he cautiously described it to himself, could be explored later under the right circumstances. To that end, he predicted another encounter between Paul and Agatha. Of immediate concern however was the—

There was a commotion outside on the canal-path. ÓDouwe opened a window and leaned out. Two drastically foreshortened figures were gesturing at one another. One was Lennep, of course, guarding the house. Only the top of his hat and his outstretched hands were clearly visible, the brim obscuring the rest of him. The other person looked from this angle like a small black ball.

'Who is it, Lennep?'

Judith turned her face up towards the window. 'Get this animal off me!'

'Do as she says. Wait there, I'm coming down. Wait there.'

On the way down, he arranged his thoughts, calculated a diversion with his man, considered some lies, straightened his hat and pulled his gloves tight. Downstairs he saw that she already knew about Agatha. 'Why did you tell her?' he barked at Lennep.

'I didn't, sir. I told her I'm not allowed to say…'

'I want to see her,' said Judith.

'Who told you, then?' said ÓDouwe.

'Jacob.'

'Who?'

'A servant here. He came to see me.'

'Why?'

'Why? Why do you think?'

'Alright, come in.'

'Where is she? Upstairs? Let me pass.' Judith tried to push past him.

'You must be calm.'

'Must I? Why?'

Why, to establish a bond, even if only of pain delivered and received. A sacrificial bond, with Judith's grief substituted (or diluted), and an end to ÓDouwe's detachment – an office requiring exhaustive precision. Or to establish a supremacy – of municipal derivation if need be, because in conceding to that much, she must also concede to the man, for who could say where one ended and the other began? 'Because you must,' he said.

She responded with unexpected solemnity. He panicked that she had divined his meagre purpose. The solemnity persisted, absorbed in its own calculations, and solemnly, as if ending a prayer, she said, 'Alright.' Devotions completed, she added, 'But tell your idiot how to behave with humans.'

ÓDouwe looked over Judith's head and said to Lennep, 'Next time knock on the door and a servant will come and tell me who it is.' To Judith he said, 'I'll have him flogged if you like.' Lennep kept himself still and quiet for a moment before ÓDouwe kicked the door shut.

Judith headed for the stairs. 'Just instruct him. There's been enough cruelty, don't you think? My Father is very upset. What need have you to threaten an old man? And steal from my friends?'

She was almost running up two or three steps ahead so that his eyes were level with the back of her hair which he noticed curled in several directions all at once. 'You mean Norvell who spies on you by day and by night?' he said.

She turned and he almost collided with her. The lighting was not good just here. Her face was made up of small motile shadows.

'None of that matters now, does it,' he added, hoping that recent gains not be utterly lost.

Judith had reached the top and was fixed at the threshold to Agatha's bedroom. Agatha stood up and smiled and beckoned her in. Judith dared come forward only a few steps. A small tremor of hysteria made itself available to her, and she preferred to give its dreadful progress most of her attention.

ÓDouwe tried to peek in from outside without being seen, but he gave himself away with some noise – the scrape of a shoe, the creak of a hinge – because Maria asked him, 'Do you want me to do anything, sir?'

'Why?' he replied curtly. 'Were you intending to leave the room?' At this moment, a peculiar force seemed to be possessing all three women: they were held in each other's orbit, but out of each other's reach, and the shapes of air between them seemed as palpable as their solid selves. And he the observer, the astronomer, in their thrall, noting their courses.

The servant Jacob arrived at the top of the stairs, short of breath, the shoulders of his coat stained dark from the rain. 'Sir, I found My Lady Mistress!'

'Well?'

'Well, sir, she's just walking around town. Very fast. Around and around.' The servant was alarmed to see Judith there.

'It's alright,' she said to him.

○

Flowers at night are an eerie reminder of other worlds. More so if they precariously adorn the lid of a coffin being dragged without proper ceremony into the middle of a town-house courtyard.

A rite was surely indicated, without which… admission of gross error. And who was supposed to face the carpenter and acknowledge the absurdity? Or was it that one coffin too many had been unaccountably, blasphemously, produced that month, so that the surplus should be returned to its prime and sovereign maker?

The purposes of the gods being at all times too obscure for any reasonable response... Hence, larger-than-life gilded scythes, corn-baskets bearing divine infants, visions of Eternity consisting of stable weather and reliable crops – dense agglomerations of obsequy induced by confusion. Or at the very least, as on the present occasion, a floral arrangement impetuously pilfered from an occasional table.

'Pull it. No, push it.'

When the coffin passed through the great van Bosvelt halls, the old ghosts in the portraits animated by the flames of the lamps followed its progress. No-one had troubled to turn them to the wall, though one mirror had been hastily covered as a small concession to established custom and perhaps also to limit the scope of the deed – because mirrors multiply.

The lamps lit the coffin unevenly and threw crazy shadows onto the ground.

A trumpet sounded and a bell tolled, but these were only the signals given by the Authorities to announce the passing of another hour on Earth.

Lennep, feeling bored and superfluous, using the excuse of the rain loosening his grip, let go of his end so that the others lost balance and dropped the coffin onto the bricks. ÓDouwe was standing off to the side. 'Is there any time when you're not stupid? I bet you're even stupid in the middle of the night when you're asleep.' The others laughed, and Meer gave Lennep a sly kick.

'Turn it,' ÓDouwe ordered them.

'What?'

'Turn it to the east.'

A religious scrap salvaged or misplaced in these circumstances, hard to tell, but they obeyed and began to drag the coffin around.

'Burn it,' ÓDouwe added.

'Turn it or burn it?'

'Wait.' ÓDouwe went inside and fetched a hot peat still enclosed in its footwarmer. 'Here, put this inside.' He grabbed the flowers from the lid and, in doing so, launched a glittering arc of droplets. There had been a general curiosity about what was in the coffin, soon to be satisfied. Meer lifted the lid. Except for a few bloodstains on the lining, it was empty. ÓDouwe tipped the smouldering peat into the vacant space. It sizzled minutely in the saturated atmosphere, but the wind still managed to awaken a glow on its surface transforming the humble object into a parody of a human soul, ambiguously heated and lit.

'We need more kindling if it's to catch, sir.'

ÓDouwe was not ready to respond. He had stepped back out of the orbit of the lanterns. Finally he spoke. 'Bury it.'

'What did he say?'

'Put the lid back on and bury it as it is. Right here. Pull up these bricks and start digging. Go and fetch spades.'

'Hurry up,' said Meer to one of the servants, 'it's starting to smoulder.'

'Take it out!' someone said.

'Throw some earth on it!' said someone else.

'What with?'

'Where from?'

'Over there!'

'Look it's catching fire! What shall we do, sir?'

Lennep ran forward pulling a bottle from his coat and poured some of its contents onto the flames.

'What are you doing, you idiot?' yelled Meer. 'Make sure you know that's your share, not mine.'

The servant reappeared with some inadequate looking gardening tools. 'What are we supposed to do with those?' asked Lennep. 'You can do it if you want. I'm not.'

'Let them do it,' said Backer, referring to the house-servants. 'It's their yard.'

'You'll all do it,' said ÓDouwe. 'Take turns.' He shook the bunch of flowers at Lennep and Meer, releasing another miniature constellation. 'You two first.'

They scraped at the bricks and sweated and cursed for several minutes until one was free. 'Get out of the way,' said Meer to Lennep.

'Well it's easy now I've done all the work,' replied Lennep.

After watching them for a while struggling to scoop the moist stubborn earth away, pausing for breath, wiping the sweat and rain from their foreheads, ÓDouwe said, 'Let someone else have a go. And throw some more dirt on that fire. It's starting up again.' The servants meanwhile looked at the ground dubiously. 'Get on with it, you bloody women!' ÓDouwe barked at them, and they fell on their knees and scrabbled at the bricks and dirt. The other employees of the van Bosvelt household muttered prayers under their breaths.

High above them, framed in two separate windows, softened by the drizzle, Mrs van Bosvelt and Agatha watched their progress.

Time and again, ÓDouwe changed the teams over. The ground was denser than expected and the tools weren't designed for the job, so that two hours passed before they could even stand up to their knees in the grave. All were exhausted and in danger of losing heart. Progress was slowed further when Meer, with ÓDouwe's permission, and against the protests of the cellar-keeper, gained the key from him and brought them several bottles of good foreign wine.

'That'll do,' ÓDouwe finally declared. 'Get it in the hole.'

'Will it fit?' someone asked.

They dragged the coffin to its final resting place and pushed it in, but it protruded several inches out of the ground at one end, which gave rise to fresh bickering.

'Alright, alright,' ÓDouwe said, transferring his impatience to the flowers but restraining an urge to shake them again.

'What shall we do with the bricks, sir?'

'I don't know.' He tested the edge of an idea to set them on top of the mound, felt its wrong comic harshness. 'Collect them up and sell them. You've earned it.'

With the coffin interred and a good mound of earth set on top of it, there remained the quantity of spare earth displaced by the volume of the coffin. There was a long moment of consideration before he told them to disperse it around the trees.

He grabbed a bottle from one of the servants, tilted his head back, squinted against the rain-mist, and took several long gulps of its contents. Wisps of smoke curled into the air from the mound on top of Agatha's coffin.

When they were back inside the house, an uneasy quiet took hold of them all. ÓDouwe threw the flowers back onto the table he had found them on and had the cellar-keeper bring more wine.

○

Forces of a novel delicacy would be required. The rumours were already circulating by word of mouth and in the Press, but only the will of the Superintendent Bailiff could be allowed free range. It alone, rumbling inside the Assistant Superintendent Bailiff's head, could be relied upon as gauge for the various peculiarities of the case. Random trajectories of the herd, or of Agatha's will, or that of her staff, or indeed ÓDouwe's staff, must be headed off. The last thing he needed was a comic entourage.

Agatha's face which he had been silently glaring at for some time was by contrast a simple matter: young, smooth, round, pink, uncomplicated by her former woodland strategies of alarm against intimacy. She turned away, by now used to these habits of his, to check the effect of the make-up her servants had for some time been applying to her face.

ÓDouwe spoke to her reflection. 'I used to think a person wasn't worth talking to unless he had a smashed nose.'

Agatha considered her flesh: 'But I haven't.'

'Yeah, well… I see you do nothing now but pore over pictures. Is that what people do instead of being dead?'

Agatha turned her head this way and that, touching an uneven spot near her lip.

Alterations had already been wrought in the maid Oopjen to augment a pre-existing likeness to Agatha, additionally served by Oopjen's anxiety (providential reminder of Agatha's former manner) at having to wear an oppressively plush gown.

She and Maria were applying rouge to Agatha's cheeks. Every time they hesitated, thinking they had done enough, ÓDouwe indicated that they should do more.

'Perhaps we should ask the Dead,' he continued. 'Or we could ask you, I suppose.' He aimed a surprised look at the side of her head as if just realising the more unusual ramifications of this idea.

She inspected the reflection of his profile. 'Miss Craebeckx says saintliness wants to undo art and evil, and return us to God prior to any action or creation or fault. Whereas we exist in the created fault of the world.'

'Sounds dubious – from a legal point of view, I mean.'

Agatha observed the mutation of her face being forged by her maids. Ordinarily, it was nothing more than a familiar arrangement of features, a means of recognition.

When ÓDouwe finally agreed that the job was done, they all retreated to judge the result, only to realise they had given Agatha that constantly flushed look she always used to suffer from. 'Just like before!' exclaimed Maria happily. But similarity ran counter to the plan, so ÓDouwe had them apply white powder on top of the red.

Followed by the French wig from her mother's collection. Together Maria and Oopjen lowered it like a ragged crown onto Agatha's head. Such a manoeuvre was likely to stir aged memories of playing at being a silked and embroidered foreigner. And such memories, mingling densely with the present reality of disguise, tended to produce a sense of personal obliteration.

Over the rest of her, Oopjen's violet-black cape, the least extravagant in the house, with the hood up over the wig. The final effect was uncertain – an ailing foreign aristocrat, a garish whore, a pied fool – but at least for ÓDouwe she no longer resembled herself.

As usual, the gawkers were loitering outside, braving the steady downpour, interested in the carriage parked outside. Although Lennep, stationed at the porch looking wildly dangerous, was generally enough of a deterrent, the driver had been instructed to hold his own arms in high visibility. A party of children careful to keep their distance nevertheless trilled insults as they scurried past.

On ÓDouwe's signal, Maria ushered Oopjen out of the house and into the carriage, and the driver cracked his whip at the same moment the door slammed shut, and in the carriage's wake a handful of the loiterers followed for a few paces.

ÓDouwe, Agatha and Backer left by the back way.

At the edge of the Biesbosch, Backer pulled up the horse and Agatha climbed down from the cart, her clogs immediately sinking into the wet ground. As she struggled to follow ÓDouwe who was already striding ahead, she was tipped forward causing her to thrust her hands into the sticky mud up to the wrists. Backer, holding onto his battered liripipe, trotted behind her and pulled her up, using the opportunity to feel the give of her flesh. She twisted out of his grip and battled on. When they caught up with ÓDouwe, he distractedly considered the mess Agatha had so quickly got herself into, then he gestured around him. 'Do you know this place?' And when she didn't answer immediately, he added more emphatically, 'You know this place, don't you?'

She shook her head and straightened the wig with a mud-caked hand, Backer inspecting these movements at close quarters.

They started off again, Agatha trying to walk in ÓDouwe's footprints because he seemed to have the knack of not sinking up to his ankles in the soggy terrain. Backer shadowed close behind her trying to do the same.

ÓDouwe halted and began searching the area for signs of former human presence, but they had been mostly washed away except for a negligibly darker patch on the ground. 'Look here, see? A fire. You know this fire?'

'There's no fire, Mr ÓDouwe.' She blinked away the droplets gathered on her eyelashes.

'Not now, but there has been, and recently. Look at the ash.'

She and Backer examined the slight discolouration of the earth where he was pointing. 'Why have you brought me here?'

His finger remained extended. It too gathered a droplet at its extremity. He took time to ponder her question, then checked her face for any obvious sign of dissimulation. 'To stir memories. For instance, I wonder if your Mother hasn't ever ground some medicine into your soup to make you sleep, or to make you unaware of your actions, or to forget them. In order to contain you, or bend you to her will.'

'I am obedient to my Mother's will.'

'Only insofar as you know what it is. She may will other things of which you are unaware. How old are you now?'

'Sixteen…' Saying it drew a grain too much of her energy.

And the hood, the wig, the slanting rain, the mud and the smeared make-up slowed down ÓDouwe's and Backer's absorption of that number. 'That's very young. You've hardly lived.'

Backer nodded too and produced from his cloak a piece of meat wrapped in oiled paper. He turned it this way and that and pulled from his belt a knife which he wiped on his leg. He used the point of the blade to flick from the surface of the flesh a wriggling maggot. Satisfied with his preparations, he cut off a slice, popped it into his mouth and began to chew thoughtfully. To Backer's mild surprise, ÓDouwe also produced an item from his cloak, a bottle, from which he took a long draught. Backer considered then rejected the idea of reaching into a pocket for his own flask. 'Your death, for instance,' ÓDouwe said after replacing the stopper. 'Oh, come on, don't start behaving like that. Yes, death, death, death. Or your replacement.'

Backer stopped chewing.

ÓDouwe continued: 'It may be that there are two of you. Have you considered that possibility?'

Backer resumed his chewing, but at a slower rate.

'Two of me? Like my Mother, divided in her mind?' In itself, remarkably candid.

'Two of you, but not like your Mother. Divided in another way. You've never thought of it, I suppose. You may not be Agatha at all. You look like her alright. Well, a bit different, certain alterations in humour...' ÓDouwe thought about pointing at Agatha, certain parts of her, bits, features, corporal truths and falsehoods. Or indeed he could hold her hand (forgetting all this? Researching it more deeply?) so that each could measure the heft and temper of the other's fingers. 'What could account for such similarity and at the same time such difference?' ÓDouwe tasted sourness and turned to Backer on an instinct that such feelings would find an easier ground there. 'Anyone claiming to be someone would have to know all about her Mother.' Backer nodded, following his own instinct. 'Twins sharing a house, but never showing themselves at the same time, you know, taking turns.' He waited for Backer to nod again. 'The Mother has divined something of this split and been broken by it.'

Backer tried to show by a different movement of his head – a tilt, a wag – that he was pondering these difficult and interesting matters.

Alarm made Agatha appeal to him at this moment. 'What's he talking about?'

Backer took this as encouragement to reach out a comforting hand, still clutching its piece of meat, but she avoided it.

'Well, It may have no bearing…' said ÓDouwe. 'Your Parents when they separated, perhaps there was another separation, your Father could have removed a twin sister – when you were an infant, I mean…'

Backer put the meat between his teeth.

'I was ill and now I'm better,' said Agatha.

Backer despatched a tiny insect that had come to share his meal.

'Have you never felt anything, though?' said ÓDouwe. 'Something missing, the missing half? Agatha's clogs were again sinking into the mud, which substance had risen in uneven smears up her cloak until it had arrived in entrancing smudges as high as her pink, creased brow.

ÓDouwe placed his hand on his sword and was directing towards Agatha what Backer had learnt to recognise as a stare of murderous calculation. Very gently, very carefully, Backer took half a step backwards. ÓDouwe's attitude suddenly seemed to have taken a new turn: how much better it would be if the girl were returned to her former state, and he relieved of this burden. How easy it would be to draw his sword and hack her head from her shoulders and start all over again. Then he would once more have the body of a young girl tragically slain in her prime, and a crime-scene that might with a few clever adjustments be made to yield the identity of some murderer or other of his choosing.

But what horror if she came back yet again and they found themselves bound together in an appalling cycle of death and resurrection, accelerating towards some insane vanishing point, sometimes with her tardy revival failing to catch up with the efficient sweep of his sword so that he might on occasion inadvertently find that he had killed her while she was still dead… And then other unforeseen circumstances, who knows? Apart from a failing sword-arm fatigued from constant toil, the girl would surely take it into her head (still on her shoulders) to run away. So now the additional labour of the chase. Is it a comedy of the old-fashioned sort? Or a moral tale skimmed from the rank surface of the canal. She might eventually weaken: there may be some inherent process of atrophy in this system, so that together they might weaken, and together coincide at a single demise. Or she might gain power while he weakened. Imagine the purgatorially diminished returns of an increasingly burdensome weapon clutched in an ever-frailer fist. Smaller and smaller cutting implements then, down to a pocket penknife, while the sturdy creature gaily skips towards the horizon always out of reach.

Backer, seeing he himself was in no danger, came forward and spoke in ÓDouwe's ear: 'I'll do it if you want, sir.'

This interruption brought ÓDouwe out of his trance. 'What? Do what? No, no…'

'Why are you looking at me like that?' Agatha was becoming panicky. 'What are you two talking about?'

'So,' ÓDouwe said to her as if nothing had just happened, 'here we are at the scene of the crime, as it were, and you have nothing to say?'

‘What should I say?’

‘Come with me. I want you to meet someone.’

The squatters’ camp had suffered a decline since the rout of its menfolk. Many families had removed themselves, leaving only the most tenacious or needy or shiftless behind. Some of the animals had clung on too, along with the insects, miasmas and malodours. Here and there a mound of turned earth indicated the nearness of human death. At the edges of the settlement, the plant-life had begun to creep in towards the abandoned hovels.

As the three of them approached the camp, yelps of alarm sounded from the undergrowth. The women were gathering their children and fleeing into the surrounding forest. Agatha put her hand over her mouth and nose. ÓDouwe found Mrs Janse’s hovel empty. He banged on the roof with a stick, calling her name.

‘People live here?’ Agatha asked Backer.

‘Welcome to the swamp, darling. But I wouldn’t call them people exactly.’ For emphasis, he showed his yellow teeth and cackled quietly.

With genuine curiosity, she wondered how in her naivety she had been unaware that there could coexist on God’s Earth such a distinct and incompatible type of human.

Mrs Janse cautiously showed herself, surrounded by some of her surviving children. She looked even unhappier than she had on ÓDouwe’s first visit. Backer managed a grin nevertheless. ÓDouwe guided Agatha towards them. ‘Come here, Paul.’ Mrs Janse led her son forward. ‘Stand there, boy.’ ÓDouwe had Agatha remove her hood and wig, gave her a kerchief to clean her face with, and stood back to watch for any reaction. Paul and Agatha were within arm’s reach of one another. Paul fixed his morose, unblinking gaze on the dripping wig which dangled at Agatha’s side.

‘Well?’ ÓDouwe said to him, ‘What have you to say?’ He turned to the mother. ‘Does he still not talk?’ Mrs Janse shook her head. ‘What about you, Agatha? The last time I saw this boy, he had your blood under his fingernails.’

‘Mine?’ But it had not yet registered fully. The wig was the thing just now, having taken on the appearance of a sleeping animal. Glad to be rid of it, Agatha stepped forward and presented it to him. He made no movement. She lifted his hand and placed the wig onto it.

‘Her blood on your hands, remember?’ ÓDouwe said to the boy, it seeming possible that before her death, Agatha had seen this boy watching her in the woods, and together they could now give a reasonable account of the event.

‘My blood?’ Now it registered. ‘How could that be so? What on Earth are you accusing this poor wretch of? I have not bled, have I?’ She looked to Backer who gave her an ugly smile.

ÓDouwe’s was a plan comprised of specks of plausibility straying within blank acreages, and it would be pure optimism at this stage to expect a reversal of this ratio. Nevertheless, with time and diligence the specks could develop into shoots, tendrils, wreaths, the more densely to populate the acres. But without any sign of recognition between these two, how to proceed? A theory may be tested, disproved, replaced. But first, some kind of a theory.

‘He’s done nothing, sir,’ said the fearful mother.

ÓDouwe pointed to Agatha. ‘You know this girl, Mrs Janse. You saw her up there.’

Mrs Janse shook her head. ‘Up where, sir? I don’t know this lady, sir.’

One of Paul’s younger brothers scampered forward through the puddles and snatched the wig from his hand and placed it on Paul’s head. The other children laughed, but without much gaiety. A girl took it from his head, put it on her own, paraded around in it, grabbed one of the dogs, and tried to make it wear the wig. The wig slipped down over its eyes and it ran in wild circles, bumping into things – all to the further grim amusement of the children. The distraught mother screamed at them and slapped them frantically, but no-one could catch the dog.

'Can we not give them some food?' said Agatha to ÓDouwe.

'At a time like this, you think of food?'

'Wouldn't do them much good anyway,' added Backer, shaking his head sagely.

The dog freed itself from the wig and took revenge on it with its sharp little teeth, but ran away as ÓDouwe approached. He picked up the ragged item and tossed it to Backer who placed it over his hand like a glove as the boy had done.

'Let's go.' The rain was getting heavier. ÓDouwe produced his bottle again. He was maintaining a generous grasp on all available theories, none emerging supreme, all prone to improvement. 'The cart better still be there.'

Backer was thinking about putting the wig on his head to amuse Agatha.

○

'Yeah well, don't forget it wasn't the likes of me that produced me – it was the likes of you.'

ÓDouwe kicked off his boots, that's right, and leaned back in his chair the better to conjure up without the distraction of his own mass a luminous picture of a ship at full sail powering back to his damp island. The last of the day's light dispersing through the drizzle made of his downturned face an erratic series of mobile pinks and greys. A controversial outline described a cascade of man, clothes and furniture, while smoke gusted from the chimney of his hat.

And when would the blame start to fall on *him*? The bad weather vane, shoved around by high breezes, would sooner or later point its beak at him. The Superintendent Bailiff, ÓDouwe's commanding officer, would place any item (including ÓDouwe), regardless of previous use or merit, between his exalted self and failure.

In counterbalance to its master's wobbling centre of gravity, the chair cantilevered within the hairline shafts of its joints, producing familiar chords of dissent. Those glassy greens and grey-blues of his imagination meanwhile folded over, under and through one another in infinite patterns of merge and disassembly, while the froth on top of them, also glassy, beady, pearly, was profligately born, bounced around and killed off – all to be acutely bisected by the prow of that ship, with the straining of its woodwork ventriloquized by the mild crises of ÓDouwe's chair.

He reviewed Agatha, the matter of Agatha: naked on her table at once perfectly vulnerable and invulnerable – that's what death does for you, at least while you're still fresh. His finger idled around the rim of his cup drawing from it the waning hallucination of profoundly distant bells. Then there's Agatha in her makeup and wig holding her hand out to that dumb vagrant boy – alive, yes, but removed, unconsciously engaged in some kind of show. And all you need do to provide the right kind of grief is to reverse the order of these pictures. It was possible such a reversal had already taken place in his mind – were it not for the obstinate fact that he hadn't known Agatha before and could hardly be so aggrieved as to derange his sense of time like that. (In which case it was feasible he *had* known her and *was* so severely aggrieved that he had consequently forgotten this fact and reversed the order of his memories of her.)

Was she now dead, then? A suddenly pertinent question. One of his several memories reported her as dead, and it could, it must of course *be*, the latest information on the matter, although that conclusion transgressed a general law of the proportional vividness of any given sequence. But if he went to all the trouble of checking the facts, he could find only necessarily wrong answers.

Under the pressure of his finger, his cup resumed its music. Now would be the ideal moment to drop the whole thing, get out, go back to where he came from, pack a small bag – what would he need? Money, sword, knives, cudgel, a parcel of food. A disguise? A wig? His new boots. A shave, an old cloak, a different hat…

And if she had never been dead? The doings at the slab mere delusion, that business with the coffin an error for which the carpenter could be flogged.

The various (real) bells near and far tolling the hour gave pause to his finger and made him raise his head. The distribution of pinks and greys held their broad arrangement as if it were not light and shade but some ingrained error of pigmentation that described his face.

By what power could such dreams have infected the City? Ill religion, hag-doings: Agatha's mother or the Moth-house Madam – or Judith. Perhaps a close inspection of her pictures for… spirals? Perhaps a new inspection of Agatha naked for differences between her and his memory of her…

The last note (for now) of the last bell tapered to silence. Left alone, the self does indeed float free from the influence of the others. What if he just stayed in this wheezing chair, remote from the claims of reality, drifting on imaginary seas, memory and hope mingling in infinite patterns of merge and disassembly?

○

Agatha's room had been rearranged to accommodate the others who had come to join her there permanently. She kept her bed while Judith and the two maids occupied closets especially installed for them. And with ÓDouwe commandeering the room opposite, there was no moment of the day or night when she was not supervised.

These new arrangements protected her from the unflattering realities outside the house. They also protected the people of the City from the insulting anomaly of her existence.

Judith Craebeckx's confinement here, on the other hand, had been imposed on her by a change in her own temperament which she could not easily define, though presentiment of doom and escalating delirium were factors. These she found were feelings which could only be assuaged by constant contact with the girl. In those moments when she couldn't see Agatha, her mind would unmoor itself and drift towards a shambles of emotions: slithers of bliss twisting gaily amongst ropes of terror; flushes of despair suffused with a merry anticipation of better things to come; horror and hilarity.

To the solemn accompaniment of a four-piece band, Agatha had been staring at a small picture for as long as it took the last grains of crushed pearl to drain into the base of the clock. Judith reset the clock and touched her lightly on the shoulder. 'Come and sit by us,' she said, detecting in her desire for Agatha's company a pang of her own superfluity.

But just now Agatha wanted to stay as she was, still and quiet as a mouse in front of that little picture. The obvious was busily occurring to her. She was in thrall to the obvious: a painted scene does not unfold in time, is not a slice of a sequence. No part of this brothel (she thought) – or whatever it may be – is more than a sixteenth of an inch deeper than any other part. No event depicted in it has its prelude or consequence. There is neither space nor time in a picture. That is why, in the small gap between the made-up and the real – a gap created by art for the purpose of joining the two in itself – there is a light that stands for both evening and morning, a smile that simultaneously anticipates and reminisces, a coin that induces and rewards, a table that is both a chasm and a bridge across it…

ÓDouwe experienced a queasy effect similar to Judith's when not in Agatha's presence, overlaid with a suspicion of Judith's motives and an anxiety that the game might be closed before its outcome could be known. When their paths crossed, by accident or design, each willingly engaged the other in compromise, subterfuge, dissimulation and avoidance of the key matter. Judith, for example, had ÓDouwe explain his rank and the route by which he had arrived at it. For his part, ÓDouwe had become curious about the art of painting because it seemed always attached to other matters trivial or essential.

The picture Agatha was staring at was placed at such an angle relative to the window that it was difficult for ÓDouwe to distinguish the painted matters from the daylight sheen fanning across its surface. He squinted at it for a moment before saying to Judith, 'They're supposed to be beautiful, aren't they? But a tree? A loaf of bread?'

'Or God wants to differentiate. A flaw in perfection, that's His means. From the flaw comes art and evil.'

Not good and evil? There were other pressing reasons for ÓDouwe's taking up permanent residence in the van Bosvelt mansion. After all, who was trustworthy enough to delegate the work to? Certainly not ten Brink whose interest in the matter of Agatha, he felt, was losing momentum. And he had successfully usurped Agatha's mother in the command of the few remaining servants in the house. And since one of those that had deserted was the cellar-keeper, he had taken upon himself the responsibilities of his key.

Agatha's mother refused to fully acknowledge the return of her prodigal daughter, and haunted the corridors of her domain like a bitter spirit. ÓDouwe maintained as much control of her too as he reasonably could without triggering a bad reaction, and whenever she left the house, he had her followed so that he could keep abreast of the severity of her decline.

o

John Norvell's landlord had taken to interrogating him about visits from strangers, especially the police, and would not easily accept that it was merely the usual business with the van Bosvelts which brought them here. John also found that the landlord had been nosing through his things. He was thereafter careful about what he left out for inspection. He racked his brains for the ideal hiding place for his notebooks, but could never be sure they were safe.

From the distance of a furlong or more, the faces of the three women John was currently observing (through his new telescope) appeared perfectly sharp within the circle of the eyepiece, but just now some interruption invisible to him disturbed their communion. A minor adjustment on the horizontal axis revealed the head and shoulders of ÓDouwe, breaker of all magic spells, thrusting himself forward in his chair. John scanned the other windows. Visible through one of them was Ons, a common or garden piebald cat with characteristic executioner's-cap pattern covering the top half of her face. This old creature had taken to gazing at Agatha whenever she was nearby. She was not nearby at the moment so the cat was staring elsewhere, the shape of its face broken up by the leaves of a plant on the sill. It was purely an illusion produced by the powerful lenses that made it seem as if the cat were staring directly back at him with that glassy indifference their tribe had mastered.

Now Mrs van Bosvelt appeared behind it and gripped it around its torso. After a brief battle, the cat twisted free and sprang away, and Mrs van Bosvelt placed her face where the cat's had been. Hers, being larger, was less obscured by the foliage. She produced a knife and hacked the stem of the plant until it collapsed giving John a better view of the spite on that face.

○

At the sign of The Infant Within The Cross, the pictures on the walls of old Midwife Weesp's front room bore witness to an interior monotone, perhaps within the keening range, in the woman herself: Virgin receiving news of her Divine pregnancy; Virgin holding her Child – sometimes with a naked baby John the Baptist frolicking nearby; Virgin distraught at the foot of the Cross; Virgin with the corpse of her Son draped over her knees. But she could no longer see them because of the patina of greasy soot that had settled on them, and because she was nearly blind. She oriented herself within her own house by a remote memory of it. 'Who?' She cupped a thin hand behind her ear.

'Don't pretend you've never heard of the van Bosvelts,' ÓDouwe said. 'They're all over the papers—'

'Can't see 'em to read 'em.'

'—And you knew them before, sixteen years ago. You dragged the child Agatha out of her Mother, the Great Lady Eva Pietersdochter van Bosvelt.' ÓDouwe waited. Unlike him, she was spared the ordeal of her ugliness. He imagined a small redemption in resisting the urge to squash her. 'Of course, no-one will let you do such things anymore. Not since you started bringing forth the dead. I've made enquiries.'

'God's doing, not mine.'

'God's fondness for brandy?'

She regarded the blur opposite her for a while. She recognised the larger patterns: the swaying; the head-twitchings; the sudden firings and quellings of the mind. She uncorked a bottle with a small ironic flourish. 'Will you?' she said as she gathered cups and began to pour.

He had already made his own recognitions. Her old spider hands moved in every direction but never very far, and achieved little. She seemed unaware of the life they led. Without her noticing, one might scuttle off in the direction of a bottle, as it did now, or more rarely towards a piece of food that may have been there for a day or – he sniffed the air – a week. 'None for him, though.' ÓDouwe indicated Meer standing behind him. 'He's supposed to be working.'

'So are you,' Meer muttered under his breath, and picked up a lamp, lit it and moved towards the door.

'Leave that.' ÓDouwe indicated the bag Meer still had slung over his shoulder. Meer put it on the table and slunk out of the room.

The policeman and the midwife drank the first draught in silence, concentrating on dosage.

Meer roamed through the other rooms of the house disconsolately, opening cupboards, rifling through drawers, performing his professional duties. He found in one such drawer the paraphernalia of the old woman's former trade: babies' caps, tongs, linen, those placards that proud parents pin to their doors to announce the arrival of their newborn. Souvenirs and sidelines, probably.

In another he found a couple of coins. He picked up the larger one, flicked it in the air, caught it, slapped it on the back of his hand, closed his eyes tightly and made some incantation between moving lips. He peeked at the coin, breathed a sigh of relief, congratulated himself and put it in his pocket.

He found the old woman's cot and threw the pillow aside to find… no secret harboured there. Near the bed, however, was a small statue of the Virgin with an unlit candle in front of it. He picked up the statue, turned it this way and that and held it close to his eye to inspect the features on its tiny face. Not beatific so much as implacably gazing in two directions at once due to an astigmatism provided by the painter – who himself conceivably suffered from the same defect. Meer's understanding of the

Law told him there was an error here, not merely in the boss eyes, but in the whole, though he had come across many such breaches in his career. Old people's taste, that's what it amounted to. He replaced it behind its candle.

Nothing interested him sufficiently or profoundly. His blank reactions tended towards those of an ape in a menagerie. There was a large chair with a deeply dented seat and back, probably her favourite, which he placed himself in. He put his feet up on the ledge of a cupboard, pulled a pipe from his pocket, filled it, lit it and staring into the middle distance, mechanically drew its fumes into his lungs. At leisure, he considered the case. What does an Assistant Superintendent Bailiff do anyway? Give orders, take the lion's share, say where to go next, think up some reason for it... The routine had changed lately, mainly in the reasons ÓDouwe thought up for what they would do next, not that he ever told Meer directly. His entire education as a policeman consisted in whatever he happened to overhear, assuming he understood it or indeed paid it any attention.

He adjusted the pipe in his hand so that two fingers rested on top of the stem, as was ÓDouwe's habit. He tried to make a face like his master's too – alert, cautious, unhappy, not overdoing the confrontational squint – but realised such an idea of his master was now out of date, and he widened the eyes, made the movements quicker, experimented with a snarl.

Tiring of his game, he glanced around the place to make sure he hadn't missed anything, decided ÓDouwe wasn't likely to come up to check anyway, tapped out the tobacco ash onto a nearby surface, picked up his lamp and went back down.

His return went unnoticed by the two of them because they were engaged in some kind of wrangle. ÓDouwe had gripped one of the midwife's hands. She was peering at it in alarm as if it had betrayed her. 'Surprise and delight,' ÓDouwe was saying, his eyes burning.

'What?' The old midwife was weeping.

'At the happy miracle of the second birth.'

Since her imprisoned hand could no longer do her will or its own, in compensation, with her free hand she picked up her cup and downed the brandy in it.

'Yes, quench the pain, but what good will it do in the long run?' said ÓDouwe, squeezing the hand tighter. Of late, rote procedures seemed inadequate to complex modern aims. Still, memories must be persuaded to divulge their dark secrets.

Meer drew attention to himself by wiping the sweat from his lips. Such scenes provided the highlights of his working week.

Mrs Weesp was shaking violently, more than an old woman should, shrieking that she didn't understand what was wanted of her, that she didn't remember any of the people being talked about. She wanted to make an appeal to Meer, but saw from his breathing, his posture, that it would be useless.

The hand which ÓDouwe had now forced above the lamp cast merciful shadows. He lost sight of her eyes. She – or was it the other hand again? – convulsed, and emptied the cup to extinguish the flame which burned her flesh.

In the blackness that followed, trains of thought became purer. Mrs Weesp nursed her wound in the womb of the dark. ÓDouwe gave himself up to its simplicity, accepting it, prematurely, all too hopefully, as a resolution of infinite perplexities of shape and substance. Five seconds in, worryingly out of his depth with such a quality of darkness, Meer pawed his way around the room in search of another lamp. He found one, lit it and laid it on the table, where it revived for ÓDouwe those same perplexities as before, now adjusted for compound disappointment.

Mrs Weesp took a long draught from the brandy bottle, then poured some on the angry red patch on her hand.

ÓDouwe indicated to Meer to bring over the bag. When ÓDouwe opened it, Mrs Weesp whimpered, tried to force her useless eyes to register its awful contents, but all that emerged from it was a folded piece of paper, which the policeman carefully unfolded. He slid it across to her.

'I can't see it. What is it?'

'I've anticipated that. I've had it copied in a very large hand. Here, use this.' He pulled from the bag a magnifying glass.

Mrs Weesp peered through it. The glass made monstrous her pink squinting eye.

'It's a simple declaration. It won't cost you anything. Not even the ink. I've brought everything.' His hat slipped forward as he searched in the bag's depths for the necessary items. Midwife Weesp's hand made another stealthy movement towards her bottle. ÓDouwe laid the pen and ink on the table, and straightened his hat. 'Sign here.'

'What does it say? I can't see it.' She tossed the magnifying glass aside.

'It's one of the tests for devil-worship.' ÓDouwe laughed.

Meer glanced at his master, then at the document.

'It says,' said ÓDouwe, 'that you delivered of Mrs van Bosvelt a second child one hour after the first. It says that Mr Theodor Davidszoon van Bosvelt, husband to Mrs Eva Pietersdochter van Bosvelt, took the second child away. It says, by omission, that you are not a damned witch who must burn alive before the good people of the Virgin City whom you have affronted. Sign here, where my finger is.' He turned to Meer. 'Well? Anything upstairs?'

'Just more stuff like them.' He nodded in the direction of the pictures on the walls.

'And what did you steal, pray tell?'

Mrs Weesp was dejected anew, lifting the quaking pen from the paper. 'Why should you steal from me?'

They ignored her.

'Not much,' said Meer to his master.

○

'Bit higher.'

Meer straightened up, easing his weight off the bar, and shifted the flattened end of it up a couple of inches against the join between the door and the jamb. Backer raised the heavy hammer, a long-handled twenty-pound block of metal, and swung it towards the protruding end of the bar. As it made its clanging contact, Meer averted his face. The angle of attack was imperfect and sparks mingled with the rain. 'You want me to do it?' asked Meer.

There were muffled exclamations from behind the door which they ignored.

Faces appeared in neighbouring windows. A few pedestrians paused to see what was going on, but the policemen ignored them too.

'Just hold it still.' Backer raised the hammer again and swung it again and this time made good contact, splitting the wood of the door vertically from the tip of the bar. He swung one more time and drove the bar deep into the split.

'Who's there?!' barked voices from within. 'Stop that din!'

'Stay back!' shouted Backer, adjusting his liripipe and wiping his forehead with his sleeve.

'One more,' said Meer.

Backer struck a third time and the bar split away pieces of the door. He rested the hammer-head on the ground while Meer vigorously worked the bar until the edge of the door tore and compressed around the impacted area.

'What's going on?!' A hubbub was rising inside the house. 'The Christians are at rest! Only the jackals and heathens are abroad disturbing the peace!'

Meer put his mouth near the split. 'Stand back.' His voice lacked all urgency, as if children were in danger of being splashed with lukewarm water. He twisted the bar out of its crevice and stood to one side. Backer was ready again with his hammer. He aimed at the damaged area once, twice, each blow reporting like a pistol-shot and sending a violent shudder through the whole fabric of the door. On the third impact, the door gave way and sprang open. Huddled together just the other side of it were John Norvell's friends. Backer and Meer shouldered their tools and sauntered in, their boots crunching on the debris, water dripping from the hems of their coats onto the tiles.

'Who are you?!'

'Who are they?!'

'What are you doing here?!'

'What do you want?!' The philosophers all talked at once.

Backer chose the nearest one at random – ben Bezalel: 'Shut your mouth.'

The philosophers parted to let the intruders pass towards the table onto which, with no regard for the fragile crockery, they dropped their tools.

'What do you want?' Fleurant asked again.

'What do you want?' replied Backer.

'What do you mean?'

'You don't want to abandon John, for instance, do you? Where is he? Upstairs?'

How am I doing? he might have added, guessing this mission promised some preferment for himself over ten Brink. If so, there was the risk of failure, fuck-up. He might want to think in terms of models, precedents, even a definite impersonation… How am I doing as ten Brink's understudy? How to ask such a thing? Do I remind you of someone, gentlemen? Am I as unpredictably brutal as him? How's my humiliation of you? In terms of style, I mean.

'You had a naughty plan,' he said, 'to abandon our good friend Mr Norvell and not pay Mr ÓDouwe the money you owe him.'

'We've been through all that,' said Fleurant. 'We don't owe your office any money. It's nothing less than theft. I have been in contact with a lawyer.'

'I know. We saw him. He's changed his mind.'

'We are scholars, religious men…' said Erlach, the big German.

'We're not. Give us your money, you deutsch cunt.'

And he had more to say than ten Brink – especially about all the peculiar relationships within the Bureau. For instance, ten Brink's bogusly attained seniority, based on what? greater age, earlier arrival. An improved scheme of rank: Meer in Backer's place, Lennep in Meer's, and a farm animal instead of Lennep. Which would mean… a marked dilution of brainpower followed by spiralling professional error, followed by blame. And Meer as Backer? Just now, he was untidily draining a horn of wine he'd found amongst the books: a man without measure. Meer's terms for the present mission would be what? Move in for a week, humiliate them beyond endurance, drain all resources, fetch in whores, cause enough mayhem to make it easier for them to run than to stay.

'Go on, give us your money.' This was Meer (practising his own mimicry?) He approached Burn and embellished with, 'Scotch fuck'. And yes, Backer was put in mind of ten Brink's sullen art: his spartan economy of swooping brutalities, verbal enormities, dire silences.

'That's what you're here for?' asked ben Bezalel.

‘Sure. Why else?’

‘What will you do if we don’t give you our money?’ asked Troost.

Backer chose a book among the many, a heavy one, gold-edged, expensive, flicked through it and tossed it on the fire. Troost rushed in to rescue it, and Meer deftly cut him on the thigh, hissing pleasurably as he did so. Backer wondered if their superiors’ absences might not tend to bring improvement, after all, as much as collapse.

Troost didn’t notice the cut. He grasped the flaming book, blew on it, shook it, slammed it on the table. Meer chuckled at these antics. The others were ashamed and afraid. Ben Bezalel, seeing blood seep through Troost’s coat, went to him, hand outstretched, but then hesitated, put fingers to lips instead. Only now did Troost feel the wetness. He touched the spreading red patch, frantically pulled his coat up to examine the wound, gargled like a child waking to the dread reality of vulnerable flesh, pressed the wound with his bunched-up coat-tail, and hobbled towards the door.

But Backer was in the way, shaking his head. ‘Allow me to quote Sumptuary Law. There’s too many of you, and you’re always here at your feasting. And now that we know where your criminal HQ is, are we supposed to let you go off elsewhere and then have to chase after you all round town? Exhausting. And expensive. Could you bear the expense? I doubt it. And we don’t want to keep coming back all the time, so we’ll have John do the collection and one of you do the delivery – we know John doesn’t really like to go out too much any more. He should be an example to you all. Oh, and you have to pay us for turning up today and doing all this work.’

‘What about the front door?’ asked ben Bezalel.

‘That’s what I mean. And this.’ Backer turned to Meer. ‘Is it bad luck to pull a Jew’s beard?’ He grabbed a handful of hair at ben Bezalel’s neck.

'No, it's good luck, I think,' Meer said quite seriously, but then decided to consult ben Bezalel. 'Is it?'

They were appreciating the universal nature of fun, its general applicability, its dependable revenues of swirling humour when John Norvell appeared, matted, filthy, darkly ringed, a fly erratically orbiting the scarecrow head – a testament to sordor.

'They stabbed me,' said Troost, blood-caked hands still pressed to his leg.

'They broke the door down,' said Fleurant.

'Did they?' said John blearily. 'Why didn't you just let them in?' ÓDouwe's agents were his agents too, viewed from a certain angle… Hierarchies mutate, cause becomes consequence, power can overheat and dissolve and then cool and set into fresh patterns. Friends, by the same token, may become enemies, or victims. Who could blame a man at the eye of such a storm for taking refuge in a turret?

All the while, Burn was keeping his eye on the tools lying amidst the broken crockery. Using the distraction of John's arrival, he moved, saw that Backer saw the movement, fractionally changed direction, put his hand in his coat, pulled out a purse, offered it to Backer (who detected in Burn's pinched dark face no sign of wayward intention), swung his fist as Backer weighed the purse – now detecting no more than a compression in the air prior to impact, snapping his head back, liripipe dislodging, teeth biting tongue. With fluid action, Burn grabbed the metal bar and swung it at Meer who was looming fast at the flank. Meer raised his arm, but there was unexpected force behind the blow and he felt the weight of it cracking on the bone, causing him to howl.

'No violence!' came a plaintive cry from one of Burn's friends.

The return swing, also unexpected, caught Backer low on the leg producing a deep, full agony around the boiling surface of which all thought evaporated – except a rueful insight that the lovelessness he was suffering would be true for anyone in a similar situation.

Using the momentum the bar had gathered on its rebound from Backer's leg, Burn launched it at Meer. While most of its energy was dissipated in its clash with the wall, a final rogue twist caught him sharply on the ribs as Burn himself, node in an equation of violent motion, nothing more, flitted from the room.

Had there not been clues in his attitude? A warning intensity, a rebellious pressure building around him? Possibly Backer had edited it from the general picture, as embers on a carpet might be ignored, supposing the responsibility to be someone else's. He felt the clammy onset of a downward revision.

○

Ordinarily, Agatha and Judith drifted within each other's orbit requiring only the occasional sounding – their utterances seeming to ÓDouwe to have little more significance than that – to ascertain proximity. But their unusual stillness signalled something novel: a plot perhaps, or a pact – an impression augmented by a cloud passing over the sun, making them seem like they were frowning at each other.

'A thousand years from now?' said Judith.

It was hard for ÓDouwe from this distance to make out all the words, though he was newly familiar with that particular span of time.

Oopjen was also interested enough to look up from her sewing.

Agatha uncomprehended the chasm. 'Will the world last so long?' She scanned her prison. 'Things will be better.'

'Men might fly. Machines that fly.'

'Giant birds, made of wood, like jachts in the air. No, that's silly.'

Oopjen found herself all at sea in a self-devouring world of mechanical devices. Substitutes for canal-boats, horses, bricks…? She giggled.

'Five thousand years from now, if you prefer. What then?'

'Wars on mountains.'

'Rivers of milk.'

'Vast cities dedicated to a single purpose, like pottery or sword-making. Storms filling ravines, quenching the furnace under the Earth.'

'Babies that learn the arts of music and painting when they're a year old.'

'Or are born telling us their thoughts from when they were inside,' said Agatha.

'Days like our dreams,' said Judith, 'and sleeping we visit the planets where kings and queens reside.'

'And savages told about Jesus,' added Oopjen with a dreamy smile on her lips.

ÓDouwe was by now sitting unusually still in his own chair, the one exactly aligned with the two open doorways – his room, their room – but turned at a slight angle to mitigate the stark unblinking immutability of his vigils. So still was he that Judith eventually came across to investigate, even wondering if he might be dead, and wondering from what mysterious cause. A coruscating rash of irreality? A murderous dose of absurdity? When she approached him, shakily reaching out to him, he stirred and breathed. She withdrew her hand suspecting that his charade of seeming death had all the while been an invitation to her. Ignoring any such possible content of her arrival, he craned around her to make sure Agatha was still visible to him. He was relentlessly repetitious on this matter of supervision. So Judith had also assumed the repetition, the insistence and the tedium of it in place of any sense of vigilance of her own. Her sigh indicated both sacrifice and relief, losses and gains – binary forces characteristic of all her bouts with ÓDouwe. His crazy theories of time and life were a danger not to the rational achievements of their age so much as to Judith's own crazy theories – or spiralling mental impulses. It was stasis, a frozen state of mind, an island of normalcy hedged all around with nothing whatsoever, that she craved and which their incarceration supplied to some degree in symbolic form.

'Sooner or later, I'll leave you alone, and all thought of you will fade from my mind,' said ÓDouwe. 'I'll go back to my usual business, which as you also probably know is to do very little as profitably as possible.'

How to reply? That such a decision in itself cannot precipitate the necessary changes in the world. Or that, in the absence of contrary evidence, it indeed might? That wistful sincerity and fond hope are not good signs, but bad signs – of further decay and breakdown.

'Do you know how many people I have killed?' ÓDouwe forced a chirpier tone, but he had the look of a man searching a bunch of keys with his fingertips trying to recognise the right one by its minimally unique profile.

Before committing herself to a response, she wanted to understand his purpose, even if that turned out to be merely to give sway to the nagging processes of misery.

'Thirty, or it could be forty,' he went on. 'The truth is I don't know. Many. And when I finally quit this job, my replacement will take up where I left off and kill many of his own. And yet no-one hunts us. Sometimes I dare to think that all these killings are making no difference to all those killings!' He gazed into the smouldering bowl.

Judith stole a glance at the aperture to Agatha's room. The musicians were playing a merrier tune which penetrated to ÓDouwe's room in a subdued register – perhaps because of the distance, or the impediments of wall and furniture. Agatha had returned to her original position prior to their game, hunched in front of the small picture on its easel, her hands stowed in her lap. She was again scanning the picture with a prodigious thoroughness, now metronomically, now trippingly, side to side, up and down, here and there: how to formulate and imprint a simulacrum of the thing in the mind; how to gather information; how to synthesise the information; how to derive pleasure from looking at a thing whose purpose is to give pleasure in being purely seen.

'So one more or less,' ÓDouwe shrugged, 'what difference can it make?'

Was he talking about killing? Killing Agatha? Judith? Himself?

'I only smoke when I'm sad,' he went on. 'And today I'm sad. Have been, in fact, ever since the moment I saw that wretched child in the woods. But it's a purely selfish emotion. My view of the world has been disturbed. And that's why we have tobacco, to redress the balance of the humours.'

'I wonder…' began Judith, but only in order to see how his face might legibly shape itself around an answer. She wasn't ready to abandon herself to his musings, but she recognised he had trapped her. He was demonstrating his power to withhold information from her. A low trick, an immature trick.

'You wonder what?' he said, all wide-eyed to show he wasn't fooled by *her* trick. 'Yes, now I'm unhappy with everything. Now I see everything differently and out of its place. The taking of people's money so they don't have to suffer the presence of their children, that's the schoolmaster's job. And painters make their mysterious visions while the corpses pile up outside their doors, one after another without cease, without hope of respite. For if they are not killed by madmen, they are killed by lawmen, and if they escape both, they are killed by God. Sooner or later. You see how melancholic I've become?' Now he was an actor, used to being appreciated, folding a note of acknowledgement into the oration.

'You've discov—'

'What's that?' he said sharply, fearing outmanoeuvre.

Judith cleared her throat. 'You've discovered that your life has been devoted to nothing.'

'Nothing?' ÓDouwe gazed at her. 'You know, you're not really modern at all, are you. You're from a past age: small head, heavy lids, bent nose, high small chin. You see? I too have been looking at pictures. A minor character in an old hell scene, perhaps.'

Judith allowed him to silence her in this way.

'But Nothing, you say?' Punished, ÓDouwe enlivened his tone with a nuance of discovery, of delighted surprise. 'That *is* how it feels. I think you've hit the nail on the head. Nothing. Yes, that's what I'm staring into right now. A very large and depressing nothing. And who has drawn away the curtain on this terrible reality? The answer is not necessarily as simple as we may think.' His eyes drifted over Judith's shoulder towards Agatha. After a pause artificially loaded with thoughtfulness, he continued. 'Apparently these bad emotions produce beauty also. Is that what painters mean? But a feast on a board like the one I ate last night? Are the tables in pictures altars and the foods sacrificial? Painters paint for people who don't paint. Predikants preach to housewives. Policemen punish breakers of the law. Slaughtermen kill lambs. There's imbalance in all that. Not like for like. But how else could it be? Like this? With an empty coffin standing in for a corpse?'

They were interrupted by Backer who limped towards his master and came to an unsteady halt in front of him, a small puddle of rainwater forming around his boots. His report consisted of nothing more than a raised eyebrow.

'You bring her?' asked ÓDouwe.

Backer wagged his head. They all looked. There was a bundle in the shadows, wisps of steam rising from it. It shuffled forward and revealed itself to be Mrs Weesp, the midwife.

ÓDouwe said to Judith, 'It'll be easier with you than without you.'

'What will?'

‘The nurse’s examination.’

‘Of what?’

‘Agatha.’

‘What examination?’

‘Of her virginity.’

‘What for?’

‘What for? I deem it necessary. In my official capacity.’

‘That’s what all this other nonsense has been about? To soften me up? Confuse me? Make me feel sorry for you?’

Or to insult with the idiot simplicity of the subterfuge, to use up anger in advance. ‘I deem it necessary.’ He had been juggling possible outcomes, meanings. For instance, would this examination bind him to, or distance him from, the corpse of… former time? If intact, Agatha is now as she was then, and nothing is learned. But if she is not intact, the test, while not providing proof of a substitute person, might establish in his mind an expansion of space between two versions of the same girl so that the first one, pre-death, could be erased from human memory and indeed history. The mysterious disappearance, unnoticed, unremarked, of virginity, might illuminate the greater mysteries of her life. If time can be rended here and there in modest manner, it can be rended in gross manner too. Who can infallibly catalogue an entire life? Who can form an unbroken thread from the present all the way back to birth? A life is made of fables, some flatly false, conjured from brain fevers or bad humours or the random filling of blank spaces in the memory. In fact, in the matter of a history of a person, reason need not apply at all. It was just that in the case of Agatha, too much lack of reason had been applied and the balance had to be restored by an artificial application, as it were, of super-rationality.

From behind the curtains that enclosed her bed, Agatha watched the mobile aurora from a lamp followed by two or three shapes. She put her eye to the gap in the curtains. Midwife Weesp was behind ÓDouwe. Each looked like the other's shadow. Nearby, Judith held herself stiff as if ready to catch them if they fell. Maria was fixed at stage left. 'You're on his side!' Agatha wailed at Judith.

'No.'

'Make them go away, then!'

'It'll be quick. Then we'll get rid of them and forget all about it.' Thin-lipped, she added, 'Don't be afraid.'

Agatha began to weep gently. 'But why?' And to ÓDouwe she shouted, 'Why should I?'

Backer, hovering at the doorway, shifted the weight on his bad leg and Judith, catching the faint creak, hurried to the door and slammed it shut with a resounding bang.

The nurse stepped out from behind ÓDouwe. An oddly shaped boulder rolling across the floor might have produced the same impression. 'Come on now,' she said, 'be a good girl.' She fumbled at the curtain and ÓDouwe pulled it away for her. Her bandaged hand accidentally flapped onto his. He recoiled from its papery fragility, but also from the indelicacy of the gesture: that horrible hand was his agent. 'Bring more light,' said the nurse.

Agatha, ÓDouwe noted with some interest, was blushing deeply.

Judith took ÓDouwe's arm and guided him across the passageway into his own room, closing both doors after her. 'She's a virgin. And if she weren't, so what?'

'You can pretend if you want,' said ÓDouwe, 'but there's a mystery to solve – the missing days. I've already examined her.'

'When?'

'When she was bloody well dead, for Christ's sake, since you must ask. She was a virgin then. She hasn't been out of the sight of her maid or one of us ever since.'

'What does it mean, even so?'

ÓDouwe seemed to be summoning up some infernal energy which might fuel his explanation, but he was interrupted by the nurse who had finished her task. 'Intactus est,' she announced.

'Are you sure? I'll check myself. No, you go, Judith.'

Judith put her hand back on his arm.

'But look at you!' he said to the midwife. He was not satisfied with this outcome: it lacked clarity, it lacked sufficient force. 'You're drunk. And blind. How could you see properly? There wasn't enough light.'

Judith asked the old woman, 'Are you certain?'

'I swear it, madam.'

'The Devil.' ÓDouwe strode up to Agatha's door and halted. 'Hag, what have you done to me?'

The nurse held up her index finger, wagged it a few times, and laughed quietly.

'Pay her and let her go,' said Judith.

ÓDouwe pushed the door. Agatha was still behind her curtain. He turned on Maria. 'Well? What happened?'

Maria's face flushed as she mumbled the few necessary details.

'I don't suppose you remember that old woman, do you?' he said to the curtain.

○

Judith's departure from van Oelst's painting school, van Oelst's reclusiveness, his narcissistic ballets, his uncontrolled menagerie, the uncivilised economy of it, the severe decrease in clients, the madness in the studio that Cornelis was deputised to oversee… The list may end there for now, but it may not always.

‘Where is he?’ asked one of the boys.

‘In there,’ said Cornelis.

‘What’s he doing?’

‘I don’t know.’ Cornelis paused at the doorway. ‘We’re going up now.’

The renowned painter Gerrit Van Oelst didn’t seem to notice him, just grunted as he raised himself to a sitting position with his legs stretched out in front of him and his hands clasped behind his neck.

‘Come on,’ said Cornelis to the boys as he passed Gerrit’s servant Salomon who knew to keep clear of him. He led the way to the narrow stairs that went up behind the Craebeckx’s apartment to the topmost floor where the store-room was. Some of the boys indulged in a bit of heavy stomping as they sensed the nearness of the two old men, Craebeckx and his servant, separated from them by only the thickness of a board.

The store-room had many windows, including two set in the ceiling, providing such an abundance of pale evening light (shimmering with drizzling rain) that the day seemed perversely extended up there, as if the place were much higher, say on some peak, stealing extra minutes of the sun’s precious time before it rolled into the shadows.

Every kind of thing was in there: shells, insects, carved busts, costumes, furniture, rugs, candlesticks, screens…

The end of the room was divided from the rest by a long partition wall exuberantly decorated with scenes of natural wilderness. In the partition wall was a door. The boys picked their way through the clutter and Cornelis opened it. Several alarmed rabbits scampered out, followed by a delirious kitten. Inside, it was crammed with items relating to their craft: canvases, abandoned paintings, stretchers, easel parts, etching acids, grounds, emulsions, inks, chalks, oils, pigments…

‘What do we have to do?’

‘Tidy it,’ said Cornelis.

The rest of them filed into the partitioned chamber while Cornelis stayed back and dusted down a chair for himself.

Rather than establishing order, the boys soon found that they were merely substituting one chaos for another. They picked up items at random, handed them to each other at random, replaced them at random, and made no progress whatever. In the course of this confusion some items inevitably got broken.

Seeing their folly, they changed their plan: they ignored each other and went about gathering things and throwing them out of the doorway. They kept on with this plan until the din of more precious items breaking alerted them to its flaw.

Dismayed by failure, they turned the exercise into a game and began throwing things around and at each other with a purely destructive intent.

Cornelis had been yelling occasional instructions from his throne, but realised he should do more at this point, so he waded into the midst of them, picked up some of the broken fragments and threw them at the others. This had the wrong effect and they all joined in with increased fury in a general bombardment.

Caught up in the pleasure of mayhem, Cornelis searched around for the crowning act of undoing. He thought of deluge, conflagration, tempest. In a moment of inspiration, however, he simply kicked the door shut and leaned against it.

The boys were immediately enclosed in darkness and silence. Only then were they able to hear old man Craebeckx downstairs banging on the ceiling. Glass cracked under someone's heel. Someone giggled. Murmurs rose and died. Down below, the old man stopped his banging.

'Ooh, look,' said one of the boys. A pale disc of light with blurred edges was cast onto the centre of a canvas fixed to the back wall of the chamber, now dripping with various spilt liquids. Within this disc were shapes of things. As their eyes adjusted to the darkness, they gathered round to inspect it.

Unhappy with their quick surrender, Cornelis heaved his weight off the door and opened it to see what was going on.

'Shut the door!' someone shouted.

'What?' muttered Cornelis with a note of savage warning.

'Look at this,' came the contrite reply, 'but you have to shut the door.'

'Haven't you seen one of these before?' said Cornelis. 'Camera Obscura. The light comes in through here.'

All eyes peered in wonder at the arrangement of lenses set into the partition wall. 'What's it for?'

'You copy directly onto the canvas. You put something outside first, the thing you want to copy, and it shows here in the circle.'

'What's there now?'

'Wait.' Cornelis went out, gathered a few items into a compact arrangement in line with the lenses and came back in. 'How's that?'

'I can't see it,' whined one of the boys.

'It's upside down.'

In unison, they all tilted their heads. Cornelis adjusted the lenses to sharpen the projected image on the canvas. Stillness took hold of them. The world, ordinarily divided for a boy into teeming categories of desire, was receiving an announcement from elsewhere. The bare facts of Cornelis's haphazard still life – a ragged stuffed crow with outstretched wings perched on a blanched sheep's skull set on top of a potter's stand draped in crimson velvet – were brought to the boys in their enclosure as a ghostly filtration, blackly enigmatic, perhaps with a tinge of the augural for extra-sensitive types.

Not to last forever, though, such obedience to awe. A raucous hissing broke into the silence and dispersed it.

'What's that?'

'He's pissing!'

'Me too!'

There followed the familiar bleat and rumble of herd law, during which they all urinated freely.

As piss-steam mingled with the dust motes in the beam from the lenses, the boys' skittering and yawing whoops mangled Craebeckx's renewed broom-protest. They spilled out of the darkroom and filed past Cornelis's totem, no longer a concord of oracular purpose now that they could view it close up.

Downstairs, Gerrit van Oelst was stretched out, face parallel to the floorboards, supporting his weight on his toes and fingertips. Holding his body stiffly, he raised and lowered himself several times by bending and straightening his arms, at no time letting his belly touch the ground.

Cleansings, rugged drubbings, gaping inhalations, inner and outer transformations. What for? Toughening up, yes, and zingy ripples of haleness as complementary advantages. But still, what for? Talismanic refigurings of a whole body? Some kind of a sweaty sacrifice? Or it was all brainrot seeping worldward, and he was busy trying to take himself out of the path of its flow.

Meanwhile, Cornelis had appeared nearby and was paying attention to one of his own fingernails. Salomon eased past, careful not to touch him.

Van Oelst allowed himself a final mighty heave before standing up, towelling the sweat from his skin and acknowledging the presence of his pupil. 'Yes?'

'I wanted to talk to you about my future.'

The painting master cast an eye over the novelty of Cornelis's dishevelment, noted the fans of multi-coloured dust on his clothes, the chemical whiff rising off him. 'Have you sorted out upstairs?'

'Yes.'

'And you don't call me by my title anymore?'

‘I wanted to talk to you about that, too. Now that Miss Craebeckx is gone…’

‘She hasn’t gone,’ said van Oelst tartly.

‘She’s hardly ever here.’

‘Temporarily. She’ll be back.’

‘While she’s gone…’ One of van Oelst’s rabbits bounded across the floor. They – along with one or two kittens – watched it disappear behind some boxes. Cornelis kept his eyes on those boxes while he gave voice to a carefully prepared sentiment. ‘No, you’re right. What isn’t known can do no harm.’

Van Oelst flexed the muscles on his upper arms, showing the worked veins in high relief. ‘Harm?’ he said.

Cornelis wavered. What was it again that he was wanting? Greater licence, some new overt arrangement, money? Or a provocation of further eccentricity, some novel crack in the edifice? Or what about a direct physical attack, or stealing gold or rabbits? Or a spot of killing – some pagan-style blood sacrifice in place of the hanging pheasant, the cornucopia, the glinting roemer – with the still-life table as an altar? The moment of credible threat was already dissolving.

Van Oelst interrupted Cornelis’s reflections, watched him hesitate, tilted his head to show he was watching that very thing, the hesitation, the falter. ‘But you don’t know the first thing about painting,’ he said, ‘despite what I have endeavoured to teach you.’

‘I do know the first thing,’ protested the boy. ‘I’m not so poor a student as you would wish to believe.’

‘You don’t know the last thing, then, which is much more important.’

‘What last thing?’

‘Am I thinking of your Father’s money, I wonder?’ Van Oelst began rummaging in one of the boxes. A rabbit sprang out from behind it and bounded off in search of a new haven. Van Oelst surfaced holding a small panel in his hands. 'Look at this. What is it? What do you see?'

Cornelis aligned his head with the object. It was an unframed picture of a young ape rolling a ball towards an open door through which nothing could be seen but shadow. 'A monkey,' he said uncertainly. 'A monkey playing at ball, an allegory… of futility… of folly… of the folly of learning, without… without access to a wider vision. Atheism?' Cornelis wanted to risk no more, so he asked, 'Who painted it?'

'That's your question? Really? Who do you think?'

'I don't know. You?' Cornelis read in the master's expression another possibility. 'Miss Craebeckx?'

'Look again at the picture. Take your time.'

'What do you want me to say? It's quite roughly painted.'

'Is there anything special about the ball?' van Oelst asked.

Cornelis stared. 'It's not perfectly round?'

'Or do you mean roughly painted?'

'I don't know.'

Van Oelst followed the boy's eyes as they moved from the painting to van Oelst's face and back to the painting. 'What do you know about this painting?'

'I don't know. I've never seen it before.'

'It is here in my hands.' He placed it on the easel between them. 'It is there.'

'What's your lesson?'

'My lesson, Mr ter Gouw, is this: what you know of a painting is exactly what you know of anything. What it may mean differs in only one respect from what anything else on this Earth may mean. That is, there is some slight possibility that the monkey in the picture made the picture.' He turned his back on the boy, removed the panel from the easel and replaced it in its box.

'I can control them in there,' Cornelis said weakly.

‘So much for your future, then.’

○

If Agatha were a picture of Judith, what immediate questions would arise because of it? Images are rarely bigger than the copied objects, but one might be primed by other circumstances to expect this reversal of scale. Sometimes difference is error, sometimes not. The weaker the genius, the lower the expectation that a painting might be like the thing painted. Differences are also spawned by poetic caprice – a science too murky for the statistician of futile evil…

Such were ÓDouwe’s thoughts as he fumed and brooded in his chamber, which gave on to the never-for-long-obstructed doorway framing the succession of perplexing vignettes which sometimes included, sometimes excluded Judith, Agatha and a dwindled but robust stock of servitors.

But in this case, the catalogue of divergences between image and object, though incomplete (they partook of the same genus, species, sex), was long. They differed in size, colouring, temperament, class, intelligence, experience, age and beauty. Agatha, as a picture of Judith, could only be understood as a radical poetic conception: an allegory illustrated by inscription of paradox and absence of familiar quality. By the means of Agatha, Judith’s powers – the meaning of those powers – were illuminated and concentrated. Agatha was a cloud, a thought-experiment, a wayward proposition of the pure densities of Judith’s reaction to Agatha. Such ‘reactions’ might early on have been spoken of by philosophers and other thoughtful types before disquiet was substituted by despair. But Judith was the living incarnation of the many strands of this chord. She had bound in herself the synoptic revelation of the exact reality of Agatha, so much so that Agatha, in her company, was reduced to the status of cypher or shadow or picture, her essential theme having been incorporated into Judith.

By refusing the temptation to ignore the urgent realities of Agatha, against the tide of a general decline in interest, ÓDouwe witnessed uniquely in himself – above philosophers and painters – the gall of the true observer. But as he continued to persevere in deleterious solitude, it was beginning to all seem comparable in effect to staring at a mark on a wall or a hue in the sky: more and yet more of the same.

Judith by contrast treated Agatha as if she were neither dead nor alive, neither here nor there, neither present nor absent. She treated Agatha as if she were indeed a cypher, an inscription on the ether, a thematic tendency in the spaces between the lives of others. In other words, she did her very best to train her mind to apprehend Agatha as it apprehended her own art.

At this hyper-elevated level within Judith, both life and art could speak freely to each other as they had never done before. What they had to say, half a dimension back, half a dimension forward, with the capricious architecture of the brain the only guarantor of meaning, was that verifiability was a liquid you could positively drink. Subjects and objects thus forced into unnatural proximity, produced ever more perfectly itemised agendas, miniaturised category avalanches, wrong but sturdy consonances, registering authoritatively in the half-life of the reflected light of some heavy nameless planet. Such liquid is an elixir that the whole body and soul must absorb and assimilate before its fatal properties can transform into nourishment.

And the priestess at such an altar, sometimes with the mysterious profile of her back turned to the congregation, sometimes with the blaze of her pale eyes trained on the host, or on one or other of the cardinal errors running wild in the house, or at the whole thick twisted creaking rope suspended from some infinite height, descending to some infinite depth, traversing the plane of this humble bedroom in the manner of a sky found at the bottom of an ocean or a lightning bolt issuing from a chair… what might she well look like, if not a diminutive, hedge-haired, crooked toothed, petal-lipped, miracle of a china doll standing (for sudden insight into certain highlighted aspects of her character) beside her own portrait rendered in the hale pink abundance of a resurrected adolescent?

○

Behind the perpetual veil of rain, Mrs van Bosvelt could now and then be spotted traversing the walkways of her mansion, up and down, back and forth, this way and that, and to what purpose, nobody knew. Everyone avoided her as best they could, so that she might sometimes begin to think that she inhabited an empty house, and that her meals which appeared regularly on a certain table exactly according to prior instructions given by her many moons ago, did so by a miraculous power, or else were all one and the same meal recreated over and over again as if time did not really exist.

Time existed all too vividly for John Norvell who, peering through layers of glass in search of signs of meaning in the world, found at this moment only the tedium of Mrs van Bosvelt's comings and goings.

But some inkling of purpose he had not divined in her previously, some hint of mission, though it may have been merely an effect of his own optimism, kept him persevering five more minutes, ten more minutes, by the gently hissing sand-clock.

He was using the standard experimental method of philosophy, the process of the discovery of the underlying structure of things, which begins with a hunch, and is refined by observation – for which some precise simulacrum of some minute slice of the world must be devised. Or it can begin with an observation, followed by a series of hunches about its meaning, subsequently tested within tightly appointed circumstances that erase, as if irrelevant, every other factor in the world. Or for the really determined man of reason there is always the option of rebuilding a portion of the world for no known purpose and taking a really good long look at it. Some kind of random scrying, that one, verging on the owl-brained industry of the painter. But such extreme ventures of speculation might take one away from reason back to primal states where time and matter hotly merge.

In whichever case, Mrs van Bosvelt had picked up speed and John had trouble following her as she flitted from one room to another. But he stayed with it until the meaning of her increased velocity was revealed to him: she was chasing the cat.

Ons in its own right interested John. Its exclusive attention to Agatha did not seem to be the result of an instinctual prescience of danger, because that would only make the cat flee. On the contrary, it was as if the cat were curious about Agatha, if not in exactly the same way, then to the same degree, as John was curious about Agatha.

By the same token, it had learned to fear Agatha's mother who, like a large spiteful animal herself, lashed out or hissed whenever their paths crossed. And now Mrs van Bosvelt once again had a firm hold of it as it bit, scratched, growled, spat and twisted. But despite its efforts, she maintained her grip, and though she writhed as the cat inflicted savage wounds on her hands, she would not let it go.

John lost them for a few frantic moments until they resurfaced in Mrs van Bosvelt's own room, illuminated patchily by a single candle, the grand chandeliers having remained unlit for some time. The cat's body had now become limp in her arms, though its tail still flicked erratically. It seemed to John to be not pacified but defeated.

Visible through his powerful telescope, Mrs van Bosvelt, with the cat held in the crook of one arm, busied herself clearing a space on the table in the far corner of the room. Now she placed the animal there where it remained supine, gazing up at her, its will surrendered.

She lit several more candles in two candelabra that stood either side of the table. These spread a warm light over the whole corner and revealed on the wall above them a small picture of a little fair-haired girl. The cat waited. Mrs van Bosvelt kept still in front of her altar for the space of a beat of her heart, for the space of a second beat, for a third, a fourth... And they were slow beats: she was as calmly in possession of herself as she was of the cat.

Judith's own heart had slowed in concert with Agatha's and Oopjen's as they sat together in soporific communion, with the musicians in adagio mood. Oopjen as usual was not required to speak, for she was deemed to have allowed nothing important to develop in her mind – which may very well have been the case. She appreciated her place within the ambit of her mistresses, watching her hands and the work they did, allowing her superiors' talk to breeze towards her, occasionally spiked by some scandalous or dubious gust.

Agatha drew herself away from the portrait of a young man with green-tinged lips that she had been examining at some length and turned to her former teacher. 'Being young and smooth and pink is all for to convince each other to produce the next generation. Then we change and get older and wrinkled and grey and no-one wants to reproduce with us anymore because our bodies no longer have those shapes they want.'

Oopjen was moved to exclaim, 'But you're lovely, Miss!'

'And we're each given a body, male or female, to start with, and fat, thin, in working order or lame and disfigured. And why? Because of some chance? Because of some lesson? Between the two, I think. That's why we're never sure.'

'God be praised, Miss.'

And bashfulness? By some contiguous mechanism of the mind, Judith was moved to consider this question. Might it be an extreme form of vanity? A curse, never being able to look away from yourself. A poisonous strain of egotism. Or slowing all down, making all objective, disentangling the person from the world, seeing the blind spots. Philosophy, then, in raw form. And when it vanishes? Act Two.

And Ons, Judith realised, was at this moment too plainly absent from her perpetual vigil. She got up and went around the chamber calling the beast's name, looked into the passageway. On the floor, a trail of meat. She followed it, passed ÓDouwe settled in his chair, drinking, smoking, reading.

From his humid turret, John kept watch.

The trail led to Mrs van Bosvelt at her altar. The cat was looking up at the old woman as if she were a quick movement of shadow whose meaning was not yet known. The mistress stretched her mouth and presented to Judith an unseemly leer, and the cat, suddenly free of its spell, righted itself, leapt from the table and scurried away.

'What are you doing?' asked Judith.

Mrs van Bosvelt gave a mirthless laugh. 'Praying.' She held up her bleeding hands.

'What happened?'

Judith took in the shrine, the votive candles, the icon, the knife aligned with the edge of the table. She thought of Abraham, Isaac, the Angel. But Abraham hadn't waited in patient expectation for the angel as Mrs van Bosvelt had for… Judith? And Isaac had made more complaint than the cat did, the cat that was the same age as Agatha. Mrs van Bosvelt's was perhaps a sincere, if risky, prayer. Anyone else in the house might have followed that trail. And each in a different way would have disappointed. A woman able to use such iniquitous suasion on a cat, and to summon Judith from afar with the power of a sacrificial charade – for ordination? apotheosis? – perhaps the booming din of the Lord did rattle through it all, or…

'What now?' Judith asked.

A hiss, a cackle. 'That depends on you, doesn't it?' Mrs van Bosvelt shuffled away depositing in her wake on the boards an untidy dotted red line.

…Or, mere madness, cryptologia, the dread power of sin?

Through his telescope, John saw Judith approach the altar.

○

Or indeed cryptorrhoea. John had invented a chance machine – his plan being to test the trustworthiness of common sense, or to make of a world unfurling towards infinity a binary reduction, or to unpick the secrets of averageness, or… something. And Judith was busy inspecting it. Her plan was to breathe through her mouth until such time as she had become accustomed to the odour of canal John favoured for his turret.

The chance machine was a complicated affair designed to spin coins into the air, catch them and inscribe in ink on a scroll of paper the outcome – obverse or reverse. As it repeatedly ran through its sequence, it made a tremendous whirring din. The fruit of silence then, this machine, the fruit of quelled emotion, as much as of philosophic enquiry. Discernible too a correspondence between this apparatus for tracking a random process, and the telescope randomly tracking conscious processes: both lunchy excuses for evading the truly vivid.

Red-eyed from lack of sleep, having finally achieved that particular dream, he was peering through the latter instrument into Gerrit van Oelst's attic in which the disarray had been put right. He was paying particular attention to the strange totem of crow, skull, potter's stand and velvet that Cornelis ter Gouw had built, and even more particular attention to the copy of the totem that had magically appeared on the surface of a canvas one afternoon – which John had at first mistaken for a shadow, and which was gradually fading towards a uniform greyness. Down below, John could see Mr Harmen Flinck standing aloof, gazing thoughtfully at a picture to stage left, while Gerrit's animals scurried about or snoozed in their nests.

'Rabbits multiply at a greater rate than cats…' John said to Judith. Together, their mood was weary, cloistered and ludic – that of children confined by a storm.. 'Sometimes the cats summon up the courage to kill the rabbits. Which means there's less of them to feed. And they discourage the rats which prey on the rabbits – which I suppose might be counterproductive. But no part of the rabbit is wasted as far as I can see. Glue from the skins, meat… Have you seen that absurd fur hat he wears?'

'What?!' Judith shouted over the din.

'I think he's trying to look like a Russian. He's run out of money, you know. No-one goes there for pictures anymore. Except that Flinck. He's there now.'

Gerrit van Oelst, himself formerly a man of inaction, was raising and lowering himself from a horizontal bar using only the power of his arms. The detail was terrific. Even the beads of sweat on his brow were distinguishable from the rapidly slanting raindrops outside. John considered some possible rationales for this new vigour of Gerrit's, this diminishing of the range of available interests until he got down to his own skin. He had neglected all else, it seemed, letting Cornelis run the lives of the boys. Ill-advised choice of viceroy, that, recalling comparably disastrous episodes in History. The boys in the other room, supposed to be labouring at the surface of a large painting, were chasing one another around the easels. Partly obscured by the rain, the lead cames, the buckled lights, the plant behind the lights, a section of wall, an easel holding another canvas, several chairs, and the boys themselves, John was able to discern some sense of the picture's development. It had begun as an expression of pure chaos, paint having been swirled randomly to produce a rudimentary guideline for subsequent refinement. Over the course of many vigils, the chaos had given way to forms, though following no familiar order. The trees, hills, people, animals, sea, sky and clouds seemed to disobey all rules of pictorial sense. Frothy waves rolled over clouds set in the sky, while other clouds billowed about the protagonists' ankles. That sheep was bigger than the mountain it peeked out from behind. A knight on horseback galloped upside down across the surface of a winding river the colour of sulphur. A relentless discrepancy pervaded throughout between various emotional and practical styles: the rough sat cheek by jowl with the smooth while solemnity rubbed shoulders with frivolity. History was defied, and the religious was confounded with the secular. And while some events were illuminated without guile by the midday sun, others unfolded in relative secrecy beneath a pale moon. Or so it seemed.

Such may conceivably have been produced out of the painting master's own relinquishment of reality, if not merely from his neglect of the boys – with Cornelis sidling into the gap and providing Law of an intrinsically disordered character. Any external chaos, therefore, say in a painting, might just as reasonably be attributed to forces emanating from ÓDouwe. Unless the whole thing stewed solely in the bowl of John's own head, if chaos it was and not merely order described by novel means, unleashing formidable anxieties of interpretation and as yet ungrasped paradigms.

From behind the chance-machine, Judith spoke.

'What?!' said John.

She spoke again.

'I can't hear you!'

'Turn it off!'

John came over and flicked a lever. The contraption clanked and shook and then creaked to a halt. He inspected the scroll for a moment, tapped the smeared ink. 'The document of our age…'

'And this?' Judith went to the telescope.

'See for yourself.'

Far away, Mr Flinck was tapping his cane against the heel of his boot while still gazing to the left at the large picture. It showed an unclothed nymph. 'Ah,' Judith breathed, recognising her own features on the face of the nymph. Gerrit briefly appreciated himself in a mirror, flexed an arm, watched the shadow snake along the protruding muscle, before picking up a paintbrush and touching Judith's left nipple with it two or three times. The servant Salomon went by sweeping up the ordure left by the animals. As he passed the picture, he halted to give it the benefit of his attention, but made no indication of any special feeling about it. With predatory detachment, Judith considered her own feelings. The picture itself as always provided the definitive key: how it demonstrated its own lack of urgency to exist, how it struggled to make more of something than was there. It wasn't an especially bad example of a standard exercise in prettifying desire.

'What happens in a darkroom?' John asked.

'You mean lenses, light, all that?'

'Is it the death of invention in painting?'

'It's an aid like anything else, like the straight edge, the grid…'

'But you've got the whole picture instantly there on the canvas, and all you have to do is fix it in paint.'

'Well, don't forget all the special adjustments we're fond of making. And you've got to choose which bit of the world to project onto the canvas. You know in this City there are more pictures than loaves of bread…'

'You exaggerate.'

'Cows then. What happens to a painter when so many produce so much? Specialisation. Particularisation. The darkroom gives the specialist another variation. The darkroom accelerates. Everything is concentrated and suspended in intimate contact, including the painter. The distances between eye, object, image are closed down. Slight, but it's the distinguishing factor. Actually, the device has no natural application, just an optimal one. The darkroom is good for distinguishing banalities – a triangle of grey on a curtain, an undulation in a floorboard – because it makes them all equivalent inside the pale flat, upside down, projection, before your very eyes, unlike the real thing. And someone sitting in the dark, invisible to himself, with a portion of the world filtered onto the wall as a blurry-edged circle of light, is well placed to attend to those banalities.'

'Or a portion of the world you concoct yourself and then project. Like those boys working at van Oelst's.'

'Are they being industrious for once?'

'Take a look,' said John. 'See the totem? See the picture leaning against the wall? It's a picture of the totem, but in reverse, with the lights where the darks should be. But it's not a painting. I saw it appear and now it's disappearing. It's a shadow that seems to have the power to linger. But you'll see the actual shadow of the totem falls to the right, not onto the canvas. And yes I've checked it regularly as the sun moves around. It never falls on that canvas.'

They kept quiet for a bit, the pair of them, glumly sifting through unwholesome sediments they had been careful till now to let settle. Such tact extended to any rogue tenderness felt by John, which under these stringent conditions, had to stay firmly in the egg, undeveloped.

'You've been watching me too?' Judith said.

John waved away a fly that was trying to land on his face.

○

'What you want to do is you want to play a different tune – one that doesn't sound like this, so full of other tunes, or so unspecific to its own particular arrangement.' This last bit said with long gaps between some of the words as the spirit of eloquence pumped through ÓDouwe erratically.

The musicians (not yet blindfolded) searched each other's blank faces for clues as to what he might mean. One note at a time? And in a wholly new arrangement? But as any practitioner of this art knows, we have already been provided with all possible tunes, so that any sweeping variation would of necessity not be music but noise. Is that what he wants? New noise?

ÓDouwe's own face wasn't giving the game away either. It was out of focus, turned away, shadowy, a moving target.

He waved a hand at them to begin. They whispered amongst themselves. He tutted to make them hurry up and get on with it. His hand mimed a series of instructions – stop that one, yes that one, that bit but not that bit, and slower, slower, slower, and yet slower, until bows were almost at a standstill against strings while other strings were barely plucked. The air was thus laden with a droning, falling harmony manqué which trailed, wheezed, revived, stretched…

But the door was really the main question. A series of screens and mirrors in order to carefully block and channel light and the alarming images that are made of it. Women, in other words.

When Judith had complained of the barefaced theft of some of her own and Agatha's clothes, she found that Meer, his befouling hands, were only doing the bidding of their master. But to what end? Her face expressed the seed, the root of bitterness. The intent was criminal, no doubt.

Through that narrow maze of screens and mirrors, shards of ÓDouwe, slices of his musicians, amputated extremities of those stolen clothes shot in and out of view. At intervals, ÓDouwe's face, multiplied and broken, was sometimes all that showed in the frame – for he had still to keep watch while obscuring the complex machinery of comedy he was constructing inside his chamber.

Mirrors were the prevailing theme: many mirrors. (John in his turret was appreciative of his privilege.) Judith behaved like the mirrors and screens: she approached, but only so far. She enquired, but reticently. She surmised, but vaguely.

What she saw of the women that ÓDouwe had brought in – a hand here, a torso there, the back of a head, a fleeting profile – added up to an artificial ménage, a wobbly smashed reflection of Agatha and Judith. She refused to search beyond this level, rearing at its poisonous revelations.

Which were: the gold beneath the brown, dresses carefully spliced… just so. Then a reversal. Then a tangle: yellow, white, blue-veined, auburn, pale pink, dark pink – much of it decorated with glistening highlights and swaying to the ill rhythms of the (now blindfolded) musicians' sorrowful invention.

A miserable dramaturgy of fucked up identity, with the puppet-master all over the place getting the strings twisted in his beard and bursting like a giant onto the dainty stage to make hay of the illusion – or to replace it with the disarray of his own inner janglings.

There had been quite enough sadness. In its place, the new policy of merriment, entertainment, rolling prose.

And when they – the whores or whatever they were – exchanged dresses, the one too tight, the other too loose, and put on wigs to ape each other's hair, what mirthsome frolics, what deep truths—

'What abundant shit!' Judith felt herself slipping out of character, or could feel it draining away, the agreed-upon self, the one that doesn't scream complaints across a hallway or mangle sentences meant to draw attention to laws, to specific clauses, relating to public performance, to venue and type. Her mouth bent to exhale all the hateful notes complementary to the musicians' elastic complaints, producing a fugue of perversely energised sadness.

When Agatha, taking charge, sent the request via a (male) servant that the door be closed, he returned with a fresh livid diagonal wheal across his face.

○

It may be that quietness will eventually descend on the Earth, but in the meantime…

'Why did they do it?' Gerrit was referring to those former high jinks of his pupils who stood by in the attic looking at their feet.

'Because they are precocious in sin,' said Judith. She scraped the edge of the mysterious canvas (the 'camera picture' as they called it) with her fingernail and brought it close to her face. 'Look. That easel is in the picture too.' All turned to see. There was indeed an easel standing behind the monstrous totem and there it was again in vaguest incarnation, a dirty purple, and in reverse, in the picture. Judith stared into the eyes of the crow, into the sockets of the sheep's death's-head under it, turned to the window, scanned for John's turret.

One by one the boys were taken aside and interrogated as to the precise sequence of their activities in the darkroom, and they were promised severe punishments if they failed to reveal all they knew, or invented what they did not know. As each account was cross-referenced with the others, and also with John Norvell's remote observations from his window a few streets away, a reliable reconstruction of the event was carefully built up, though with inevitable and crucial omissions of detail.

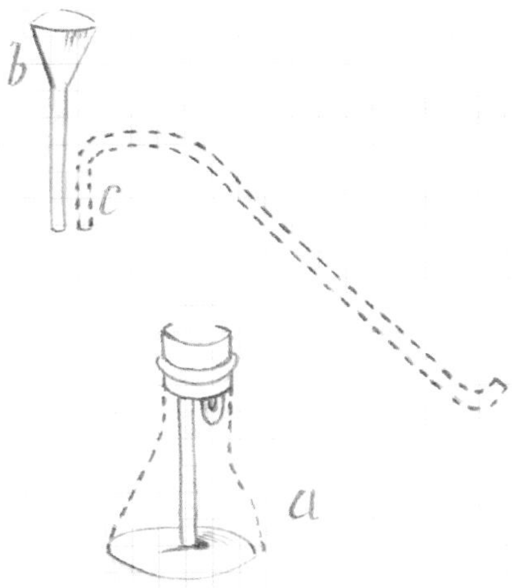
b
c
a

In their destructive frenzy the boys had been in no position to pay heed to which chemicals were spilled in which order onto the canvas.

Prior to these investigations, Gerrit and Judith had emerged from the Virgin City's Illustrious School library brandishing Latin versions of ancient texts from Arabia which contained prescient information concerning the camera obscura and its relation to light-sensitive silver salts. And armed with these books and the boys' accounts, they set to work trying to replicate the result, confident that the right combination of acid, chalk, light, glass, time and piss had produced a fixed image projected from the real world, and could be made to do so again. John was useful here too, experienced as he was in the tedious procedures of scientific enquiry. Still, no success.

Some character of their urine? They had the boys cast their minds back to their respective menus of the day in question. Had they been secretly drinking wine, and if so, which kind? Despite denials, Judith and Gerrit fed them a variety of strong drinks and collected their urine, John in charge of accurate tabulations. This they mixed with the other materials stored in the darkroom, in every combination, and applied the unguents under other variable conditions of temperature and time, humidity and sequence, to a fresh set of canvases and exposed each in turn for longer or shorter periods to the lens transmitting the beams issuing from Cornelis's totem. Nothing. At best, a smudge, a smear. Not even that much.

The missing element, the crucial catalyst was sought. Wilder and wilder theories were brought into play. Something to do with Agatha, no doubt. They lurched towards witchery, towards Agatha as anathema, incubus, authoress of dark deeds. As always, natural philosophy up to its knees in swill, its human servants failing in stamina, imagination, gumption.

'So now the dead rule the world?'

'Maybe wealth has something to do with it…'

○

'Smells like a canal in here,' said Cornelis ter Gouw.

Judith Craebeckx surreptitiously sniffed at her clothes for the reek of John. She and Gerrit van Oelst were hunched in front of their dull riddle, now removed to the back studio, no end in sight for the weary vigil. The thing was a visitation of shadows from an unknown source and for an unknown purpose – a tittery harlequinade to spice up the general hysterics. The boy hung back while the grown-ups got in closer. Salomon discreetly occupied a small space in the background.

Mr van Oelst addressed the boy wearily, as if something could be gained from a further breath of inquiry. 'This is your doing. One of your pranks.'

'I don't even know what it is.'

Van Oelst half turned to his pupil and inhaled.

'Well I don't, sir.'

'I'm going to copy it,' said Judith.

'Have you come to visit your Father, Miss?' Cornelis said to her in a strained tone.

Judith raised her eyebrows at him.

'Then why is she here?' he asked Mr van Oelst with petulant verve.

'What's wrong with him?' Judith said to van Oelst. 'Maybe it's that he doesn't like women.'

'Is that right, Cornelis? You don't like women?'

'I do.'

'And what is it about them that you like so much, that makes you so very fond of them?'

'I like…' he hesitated, curtailing any too ripe expression.

'Come on.' Judith and Gerrit showed how patient they were being.

Cornelis didn't understand the game. He grimaced sweatily. 'Well, there's a lot of detail on their bodies.'

'Too much, perhaps?'

'No, not really…' He felt the fluxus of rich chemistry that accompanies a developing thought and banishes inhibition. 'Well, have you noticed how they're totally guided by their pelvises? When they walk, I mean. There are so many more movements involved in a woman's walk than a man's. Lateral ones. Complex articulations. Rotations on the horizontal plane where you just wouldn't expect them.' Cornelis squinted at his very mobile hands while he spoke. 'I've noticed it. I've studied it.' He looked surprised and pleased, and declared, 'I've made drawings.'

'I've seen them. They're not very good,' said Gerrit.

'But then such knowledge can't be derived from the observation of clothed women,' added Judith.

'Well…'

'And what possible business is it of yours where Miss Craebeckx is?' Gerrit asked him.

'Her position here is taken. You said as much yourself.'

'I did? Taken by whom? You? He's taken your place, apparently,' he said to Judith. 'And have I been paying you your wages on time?' he asked Cornelis.

'This is the probationary period, you said.'

'Shall I start calling you "Judith" then, and talk to Judith as if she were stupid and quite, quite useless?'

'And we'll ask him all sorts of things about painting,' said Judith.

'Yes, we'll discuss the higher aspects.'

'Yes, do tell us what they are, Master ter Gouw.'

'Um… the monkey might have made the painting…?' Cornelis hazarded this error of judgement as a bid for equality, for social savvy, for self-mockery, but it hit the floor with a splat.

'What's he talking about?' said Judith.

'A monkey,' said Gerrit.

With distaste, Judith considered the bulk of the boy, its potential for insult, its gross immunity from reproach. 'Do you know the story of the ass?'

'No.'

'You are the story of the ass,' said Judith.

Cornelis wisely remained silent.

In that pause, Judith and Gerrit felt and shared a sour recognition that they had become an extraneous incarnation of ÓDouwe's method, or even less than that – his tone.

'And our art?' Judith wanted to torque the vehicle back to her own course. 'What fuels it?'

'I don't know. Light?' Two patches of pink rose appeared on his pale face.

'The story of the ass is a long and edifying one,' said Gerrit.

Judith said, 'I'm told piety of mind is essential to correct interpretation. Beware enthusiasm over inspiration. But that's for Religion, not painting.'

'Darkness, then?' said the boy, frowning into the darkness.

'The answer is Death,' said Judith sternly, while Gerrit shook his head and tutted at the boy, not entirely satisfied with himself either.

○

'What's that appalling smell?' Troost and Erlach had ascended to John's eyrie. They wrinkled their noses, seeking excuses for him: love, grief, a virulent attack of sanctity. But there was no question of abandoning him. He was ÓDouwe's agent in the matter of extortion and his master had the greater power to punish them. In another way, John had become a substitute for that tyrant: he liked of late to disdain their profound preparations for the Millennial catastrophe.

'What are you doing up here?' John replied irritably, but still he quickly surveyed his turret as it were from their perspective. Unsavoury disorder had accumulated around him – of its own accord, he thought, as in some natural process of precipitation. He inhaled discreetly, but detected nothing unusually pungent. But then he knew that the olfactory system adjusts for novel pitches of assault.

Erlach changed tack. 'Why do you spend all your time watching those female curiosities?'

'Which one are you after?' added Troost rather too merrily. 'The mute one or the small one?'

They came closer. Erlach tried to sight through the telescope while Troost sneaked a peek at the notebook at John's elbow, but John flicked it closed and spun the telescope so that it pointed back into the room.

'We're starting,' said Erlach. 'You're not losing faith, are you?'

'In what?'

'In our mission. In history. In the truth. In the future.' Their surreptitious mission being to win John round to an attitude less injurious to themselves.

'This depression of yours is another indicator of these important times,' added Troost. 'We all feel it. The burden is heavy. We are all in our ways weak.'

'I'm tired of all that.' John left the window. 'God brings us back – from where? – erases our memories, buries clues as to what to do – which is to find our way back to Him – and makes us reconstruct it all and succeed, or not reconstruct any of it and fail…'

The philosophers exchanged worried looks as he shuffled after them all the same, his surreptitious mission being to mitigate in small degree the harsh new arrangement of their relations.

'The old religions have been superseded…'

'The oracles have been silenced…'

'In the reign of Tiberius, two or three important things…'

'Plutarch…'

'…lesser deities with their own divine powers.'

'Pythagoras was a Hindoo…'

'The Orphic myths…'

'…Plato.'

'Plato was no Orphist…'

'Tragos?'

Ben Bezalel and Fleurant were warmly engaged in the usual business, and Troost and Erlach joined them with Norvell following on with a show of disconsolation.

'Don't forget the Zoroasterists…'

'Pan's corpse might have it's place in Christianity…'

'Pan is already a Christian theme…'

'Theme?'

'Pan's divine corpse, then, if you prefer…'

'Pan as a model of divinity preparing the way for Christ…'

'This is known…'

'As far as the isles north of Scotland…'

True as this detail might be in the story they were stringing together, the mention of former comrade Burn's homeland sent out a ripple of regret.

'I don't accept it. Paganism, error, that's all…'

'The old religions point back to God's original religion as well as forward, through signs, through shapes…'

'Pan's sacrifice was unique. His fate was unique among the Hellenic gods…'

'Uniquish.'

'He wasn't metamorphosed, superseded or blended into a fresh identity or dispersed among many…'

'…crucial moment in history…'

'What sacrifice? He died…'

'But why did Pan die? His life and death represent the principle of preparation, of intermediacy – Arcadian values, neither heavenly nor hellish…'

'A harbinger of Christ's sacrifice…'

'His is the first withdrawal of the gods, prefiguring the primacy of the one God, prefiguring the withdrawal of that God from routine intervention in human affairs…'

'Mithras was the one before…'

'Didn't die, though…'

'Pan's a sacrificial god. The sacrifice before the sacrifice of God…'

'He has his place in Christ's light…'

'At best, he's a worldly deity…'

'This is the world…'

And so on. John idly – or was that diligently? – watched the heavy drops of rain impact on the squares of uneven glass of the window, some bursting into smaller droplets which trickled downwards, reforming into common streams and puddling under tense menisci on the small ledges of the lead cames.

All that talk of theirs meant that according to Plutarch, when news of Pan's death reached the ear of Emperor Tiberius, he (put down his pornography and) set up a commission to investigate, which commission found plenty of evidence to support the rumour. Its effects were noted by priests of many distinct cults throughout the world who recognised by various signs the demise of a Great Soul, and that subsequent generations of Christians had discerned much meaning – because of the timing of it – in this singular event.

'You know what I think of God?' John said to them. 'Gold. Think how much of it is there in the earth in total? God is the one who holds that knowledge in his mind.'

If John himself were to excite the attention of an observer, he might reasonably ask, once again, if John wasn't now officially working for the Superintendent Bailiff's office. Certainly he kept meticulous records, annotated with personal reflections on the matters observed, in a fresh set of log books. And certainly he had reason to expect them to be removed for inspection by a higher power in due course. And certainly the money John collected from the philosophers was regularly delivered to ÓDouwe's agents. One could additionally argue that since John had quietly increased each man's quota to cover his own, plus a bit extra, that he was now directly in the pay of the Bailiff. Such appointments were always of necessity discreetly arranged. Who could be so naive as to think otherwise: that the State functioned as a simple machine, each part visible, each relation to each part explicable? No, a machine is no use as a metaphor in this case. Better to look to the world of Nature with its teeming systems of pulse, peristalsis, and humid procreation.

'Gold? Really!' protested ben Bezalel.

'As for Revelations which we spend so much time poring over,' said John, 'It's about how things are for us, for the world, at any given moment in human history. Not predictive. Descriptive.'

They waited uneasily, not wanting to argue with him in his present state. He had not shaved.

'Well just take a look at it.' He went to a shelf and pulled out a copy of the Bible, turned to the back, circled his finger in the air, stabbed the page, and read the words where the finger hit. '"...There was silence in heaven about the space of half an hour." Or here.' He riffled back a few pages and stabbed again. '"...A door was opened in heaven: and the first voice which I heard was as of a trumpet..."'

'Well...' Troost muttered.

'It's the poetry of the perennial condition of the human mind in relation to everything else. And that's what the death of Pan means as well: Now. But in a different way. Revelations aims at a constant, whereas the death of Pan points to a new age, without such numbers of deities, without any Deity at all if you like it that way. Our Age, where cold-hearted observation is the prime value, where Nature is ruthlessly interrogated to the point that its operations can be replicated at will. Old god dies. New one arrives – our one.'

As before, no-one wanted to dispute with him, with that smell, with that matted hair.

Seeing that they were not inclined to his point of view, John took off his cap and moving from one to the other, held it out. 'Call it rent for the room, if you like.' This lighthearted remark being the latest variant, amusing to no-one, on his extortions.

One by one, some with token groans and sighs, they reached into their purses.

'If the thousand years of Christ's fresh reign have to begin some time,' said John, augmenting the black mirth, 'why not now?' He reached ben Bezalel who surrendered his money like the others 'Even so, there's still the matter of the conversion of the Jews. We could make laws, I suppose. We could accelerate.'

'Kill, you mean,' said ben Bezalel, 'and force people to pretend?'

John laughed. 'Why not?' He jangled the money in his cap and headed back to the stairs.

Once more at his window, he rested his hand on the telescope but didn't look through it. He preferred to see nothing in particular, the totality. The city was made of intersecting tiers and facets: sundry, multifarious, cracked. The whole lot of it was there to accommodate the idea of separate individuals with densely personal and discrete existences engaged in ordered interaction with each other. His inky notebooks comprehensively contradicted this fable and pointed to the opposite pole: unnumbered fragments randomly colliding.

○

'No, what I meant to say…' ÓDouwe took another drink. 'Christ, what have I done now?' It may have been the state of his own eyes, but to him Predikant Lockmans resembled an eroded homunculus in the middle of a guano-covered grotto. 'I'm not really here to charge you with irreligion.'

'What then?' asked the predikant.

ÓDouwe put his mouth close to the old man's ear. 'I'm here for spiritual guidance.'

The predikant cackled.

Perhaps he wasn't joking. ÓDouwe had set out in search of something, and had perforce come to this dark place because all those years ago presiding at the baptism of the newly born Agatha of the illustrious family van Bosvelt was this person directly opposite him poised, he thought, to transform himself like a chameleon from one version of himself into another. One moment he was a tragic old man, failed as a pillar of church and community, fallen, disgraced. The next, he was a straight-backed philosopher of radical new ideas demonstrating the Reformed Church to be, like its predecessors, a toy.

It would have been preferable if this rotten priest had been some other kind of character – better or worse, but not this exactly. If better, he might have had the power to assist ÓDouwe in his quest, the precise nature of which he could not articulate to himself or anyone else. A brighter spirit might have had the power to guide.

Worse would have sufficed also. From such a one, any number of crimes might fluidly issue: the sundering of a family, conspiracy with one or other of the feuding factions, the cruellest of deceptions, murder, infanticide, and of course, gloriously, triumphantly, an unequivocal piece of satanic conjuring.

Either way, ÓDouwe would not feel himself so alone. There would be warmth, understanding, sharing – or there would be a curse not merely infecting himself as it did now, but the entire City.

ÓDouwe spun and yelled as a pair of eyes caught the light of the smoking lamp and momentarily shone. 'Who's there?!' No answer came, just a quick rustling and a fleeting silhouette, half-naked it seemed, flashing away.

'That's just my girl,' said the predikant calmly. 'Ignore her.'

'Your daughter?'

'If you like,' said the old man, showing a few brown teeth.

ÓDouwe peered into the darkness where the shape had fled and muttered the name of Agatha, perhaps as a prayer.

'I suppose I should know her, is that it?'

'You threw water on her head, when you were a man of Christ…' Now a candle floated by in the passageway, followed by the lit face of a young man. ÓDouwe worried that the vision was conjured out of his own mind.

'It's only the boy. He'll do you no harm.'

'When I was baptised in the Faith, many years ago, what did it do? What difference did it make in me? Do you see what I'm asking?'

The predikant looked away. 'I no longer do such things.'

'But you did once, and you knew why you were doing it. You knew why you did it for Agatha van Bosvelt. Admittedly she was an infant at the time. Was she ever here?'

'When?'

'No, of course not. Let me think awhile.'

The predikant watched his unease in silence, then said, 'Shall I tell you something about myself, Ollamh? I may call you that, I think.'

'Eh?'

'Shall I tell you why I'm out of the reach of a fellow like yourself?'

They were interrupted by a pounding on the door.

'Ah, I invited someone else,' said ÓDouwe. 'Hope you don't mind.' He had engineered a collision, and with the curiosity of a philosopher he wished to note every detail of impact, recoil and scattering of parts.

Backer limping, and Meer with bandaged arm, led Midwife Weesp into their presence. She was complaining loudly about the treatment she had received at the hands of these two brutes. 'They're drunk. They mishandled me. I'll say no more.'

'Sir, you told us we could hit her if she wouldn't shut up.'

'Did I? Oh well, it's my fault then.' He took the midwife by the elbow, careful to avoid the dreadful skeleton claws, and guided her towards the predikant. 'So! You meet again! Come closer, old woman. Closer still. You're probably just blurs to each other. Come on, don't be shy. Stand by him, greet him. Look what a picture they make.'

The novel elements in this encounter between strangers gave Backer an unusual thrill. Many's the time he had presented two people to one another, accuser and accused, mere characters in a play authored by his master. And more often than not they had been on intimate terms before their arrival on the stage – husband and wife, father and son, master and apprentice. But here was a curious turn-up. The stage was makeshift, the characters unknown to each other, and there had been no rehearsal. As each player peered into the other's face, offered polite greeting and made no sign of recognition, Backer began to understand that there was no set theme for their performance. They must make it all up on the spot, and his master was doing his best – 'Christ, he's more pissed than I am' – to tease from them a workable dialogue. But the theme he was so heavily hinting at was too original for them. This couldn't work. Their participation sixteen years ago at an early phase of a girl's life, that much they could be persuaded to agree upon. Each having a faint memory of the other teased out was less certain, but acceptable enough. But some meandering talk of collusion in the disappearance of a phantom twin? None of that could really take any kind of a firm hold. What was even more interesting to Backer was ÓDouwe's attempt to glue all these bits together, and the two old people's attempts – one pathetically sincere, the other ironical – to humour him.

Meer on the other hand couldn't have cared less. He looked all around him with his mouth open, and having exhausted the potential of here, he went off 'to do his job' of rifling through people's cupboards.

He came back soon enough holding onto the two youngsters.

They too were drunk, or seemed so to drunkards because of their lighter-than-air otherworldliness. Were they angels? Were they ephemera? What was their purpose? They were sages of some sect of dance, that must be it. There was something of the Kernophoric Mystery to them – the noble sheaf, the silent reaping thereof, the marriageable timbrel.

'What's going on?' said ÓDouwe sternly to them, mostly in order to bring them into a more reasonable focus.

'Please, sir,' said the boy, 'we were just saying our prayers.'

'Up to no good, more like. Mocking the Church like your owner.'

'We were just playing, sir,' said the girl. She was about Agatha's age, or older, it was hard to tell – perhaps she was even Judith's age. She was swathed in a large linen sheet. The boy, also of uncertain age, wore breeches but was naked to the waist. Neither was shod.

'Orphans. In my legal charge, Mr ÓDouwe,' said the predikant. 'Waifs, strays. What I was trying to explain before. Not many come here, but when they do, they're like you. They have enough force left in them to bring them to my door, but that's the end of it.'

'You mean I'll never be able to leave?'

'Leave what? Go where?'

'I'm here on official business. That other nonsense I said was just a joke.' He was suddenly alarmed. 'Has ten Brink been here?'

'Another friend of yours?'

'My sergeant. Stocky, flat nose, big hands, bad manners.'

Backer and Meer exchanged a glance.

'Just the kind of person you'd employ,' said the predikant. 'I should expect him?'

'No to Agatha, no to ten Brink.' Distant chimes distracted ÓDouwe. 'You're right, he wouldn't use his real name, knowing I'd be on his trail. Wanting my job no doubt. What did he say to you?'

They were getting nowhere, of course. ÓDouwe persuaded the predikant to supply powerful drinks, which were poured, it would seem, from one many-cupped vessel into another, the result inevitably being that they all slid into an ignominious confusion of the senses.

Deep into the evening, Backer, seeing his chance, roused Meer who was lolling his head in a half-slumber and leaking drink from his mug onto the boards, and they both slunk away in the direction of those captivating monsters next door.

○

Framed in each window, perhaps a different world. That one, for example, if concentrated on to the exclusion of all others assumed a reality which it would certainly be unused to. What would it make of such fame?

Through it, ÓDouwe could be seen standing over Agatha, lecturing her. She looked sullen. She didn't respond. Judith sat in her corner, watching the policeman. He was not aware of her scrutiny. His senses were not finely tuned to anything at all. He swayed as he towered over her, drink in hand, spilling a little. With his powerful lens, John could follow the course of that drop of liquor down the side of the mug. But he couldn't hear ÓDouwe say to Agatha, 'What do you remember of the kermis? Yes, the kermis. The kermis.'

Judith made a movement as if she were going to spring forward.

'The kermis?' said Agatha, 'I don't know. The usual. A five-legged sheep. A bearded baby.'

'Come on. What else?'

'Lots of pictures.'

'I mean anything unusual.'

'There was a fruit I didn't recognise.'

'Indeed. What about the people?'

'The people?' Agatha peered into her memory, glimpsed the shapes of the crowds, the flocks swirling in waves, the drinking and singing, the fighting and making up, the eating and vomiting, the surreptitious rutting, the finale with everyone crawling about having lost sight of all sense, and the whole gaudy riot mercifully cloaked in an impenetrable cloud of smoke issuing from the fires, the lamps and the hundred thousand tobacco pipes, with everyone passing into oblivion choking and fainting.

'Well?'

'Pekelharing.'

'What about him?'

'There were two of them.'

'Two clowns? What of it?'

'They were fighting – well, bickering.'

‘And?’

‘I just thought it funny – or odd. I remember I couldn’t tell if they were trying to be funny or not.’

‘Yes, yes. Did anyone speak to you? Any strangers?’

‘No, I don’t think so.’

The surface was stretching beyond its usable range, thinning dangerously at certain spots. Maria was keeping her head down. ÓDouwe’s eyes were wild, but he contained himself. Judith stood up to remonstrate with him, but cautiously, so she could maintain control over him like a big dog. He gave up and left. The women returned to their starting positions.

ÓDouwe paced about in the corridor, agitated, aimless, occasionally retreating to refill his cup.

Mrs van Bosvelt, that horrible enigma, drifted this way and that, enclosed in her own world with its special purposes. She twitched her head in the manner of a small wild creature. She perhaps had knowledge to erase: that her life was dissolving her like an acid, revealing traces of the child in her living flesh.

The paths of their restless pacing were bound to cross, and so they did with some violence.

Mrs van Bosvelt was fired by a determination to place herself near ÓDouwe. He was determined to resist. And here in summary was the dramatic realisation of their relationship: brutal, minimally articulated, antagonistic according to an ancient model (you and me; us and them; her). He found himself having to restrain her. If he were Jacob and she the Angel (that is, an aspect of God become temporarily an aspect of himself), then there was much to regret. He wished only to be free of the implications of such a struggle: that in him there was nothing but voiceless bestiality; that it had taken shape outside himself and was now in the most disgusting manner imaginable trying to get back in.

ÓDouwe's revulsion was against the capacity of madness to disturb the normal processes of power: she was a swooping crow encountered at night in a deafening wind.

John's thoughts on the matter were running along similar lines, and he was in a position to judge objectively because he could see both of them whereas they could only see each other. He too was struck by the ugliness of the struggle, by its inelegant flailings, its lack of aesthetic coherence. ÓDouwe's concern was to stop Mrs van Bosvelt without knocking her out cold with his fist. Her concern was to gain access to the fastenings of his breeches for some appalling congress. She wished to unite with him, and he keenly wished to remain inviolate.

Judith and Agatha had come out to see, while Maria obediently stayed behind in the room trying to glimpse the action through the spaces between the various bodies.

Agatha apprehended the nightmare in complete disgrace, recognising it as a demonstration specifically for her eyes. Such faults infect the fabric of the world which the brave (such as her) have made their destination, spreading hot shame.

If it had any merit whatsoever, it was as a primitive recognition of life, a natural convulsion free of mystifying preamble, an attempt to break the tangle of improbabilities. But when the forked road forks further and forks again… and again…

Judith by contrast was sensitive to the meaning of a rape attempted on the person of the Assistant Superintendent Bailiff by a female regent of a certain age. Here was a fundamental breaking of Law: meaningful consequence is not possible if madness refuses to acknowledge – even to the one it possesses – its place in the agreed scheme.

Mrs van Bosvelt's strength being no match for ÓDouwe's, she revised her tactics: loosely holding one of his wrists, she withdrew a pace or two. The edge of her dress was coming into view. One of her booted feet rose and came to rest on a nearby table like an incongruous ornament among those already there. Then a knee showed above the tide of her raised skirt. ÓDouwe broke free and ran.

Mrs van Bosvelt stayed where she was for a long time before removing her foot from the table.

○

ÓDouwe had the sensation of having just missed something – of the air being rife with the energies from some brisk exchange. Culo was sitting motionless in a dark corner. On Craebeckx's table lay a curious picture, cracked and flaked, describing a greyhound examining a pile of fruit, or perhaps a bear cautiously approaching a sleeping wolf. The crumbs and shreds that scattered out from this mysterious epicentre onto the tablecloth suggested a work being undone, a work in regress. Next to it lay the weapon, a penknife. Next to that, ÓDouwe laid the book he was carrying, clothbound, handwritten, tattered.

Even in its much damaged state, Craebeckx recognised it as his own. 'Where did you get that?' he said in an old man's wheeze.

'That Norvell boy has been keen to assist me in my important task.'

'There's nothing in there to worry about, if he has copied faithfully,' said Craebeckx.

ÓDouwe looked up. 'Copied? There are others?'

'He shouldn't have it. I didn't give him leave to keep it. It's theft.'

'But you haven't missed it till now. This is only a copy then?'

'I wouldn't miss it if I stored it where I wouldn't always see it, would I?'

'Either this is the only one,' said ÓDouwe, 'in which case, John has entered your house and lifted it, or he has made a copy of an original which is still here. Which?'

'Or I neglected to retrieve it from him when I dismissed him,' Craebeckx replied.

'What about: either these are your words in his handwriting, or it's a copy of an original and must therefore be compared with that original to be certain where your words become his words?'

'Let it be the first.'

'Let it be the second. Accept, in any case, that we must proceed as if it's yours.' ÓDouwe exhaled an ochre cloud. Feeling he had waited long enough, he said to Culo, 'I could do with something...'

Culo stirred. 'Soup?' he said and laughed.

ÓDouwe gave him a cold smile and turned back to Craebeckx. 'Why John Norvell for your secretary and not some other?'

'He was to hand,' said Craebeckx. 'He was employed by my Counsel during the Zijss enquiry which has no end. I wanted to punish my Counsel by taking him.'

'Why punish your Counsel?' ÓDouwe arranged himself more comfortably with a leg slung over one armrest.

'He was working for them, not me. Which explains the shame I now have to endure. Zijss destroyed my business, stole my money, incurred debts which I am liable for. And yet I am persecuted by the Law. Was Zijss sent by them in the first place?'

'Who knows? Has he managed to bankrupt you yet?' ÓDouwe was fond of flourishing this taboo in front of Craebeckx who duly quaked at it. 'So here you are at this ruinous brink of which we should speak in whispers. And there are all the other wicked deeds – better to bring it all out. A full confession. Unburdening, then. A full understanding of every twist in the labyrinth – from its outer regions through its fiendish pathways to the centre of it.' ÓDouwe's hand spiralled.

'What centre? Who's there? Me? Or you mean Zijss?'

'Zijss is only a part of it, but yes, there's a man I'd like to talk to.

Approach with caution, though, I would say. Approach as to a dangerous reptile. Yes, yes, it may not have been a formal arrangement, but there were hearty suppers, no doubt liberally watered; there were occasional gifts, a pair of unusually soft gloves, say, or a fur-trimmed coat. And his purpose, that's the important thing… But he's nowhere to be found, is he?' (Culo placed a cup next to the book. Craebeckx eyed it with distaste.) 'But before we get to the centre, there's a great deal of work to do. We must proceed systematically from its outer regions. It's the only way to understand the thing as a whole, and to master it.' ÓDouwe lifted his hand from the book and reached for the cup.

'Master what?'

'The labyrinth. Starting with the multitude of doors ranged around its perimeter.' ÓDouwe demonstrated this layout with items to hand: the penknife, the water-jug, a small vase (containing seasonal blooms), the wine-jug, the book. His own cup stood for the mysterious centre.

Craebeckx didn't like the way all this made him seem like an old man who had lost his grasp of the world.

'I'm trying to drain the mud out of the water, that's all,' ÓDouwe continued. 'None of it's personal. You're not the target here, but I must have your full co-operation. I'm not interested in you. You'll be dealt with in the Bankruptcy Courts,' (pause for Craebeckx's recoil) 'and if there's justice in it, so be it. If not, it must be put aside as a distraction.' ÓDouwe wagged his finger at the book. 'What was your purpose in this?'

'It's the history of my life. I wanted to set down without embellishment the sequence of events that have constituted my life up until now.'

'Vanity? There are more volumes then. This one is not perfectly up to date.'

'I told you I had to let John go,' Craebeckx said. 'And Zijss's place in my story is assured wherever I put him. I could no longer afford… His guilt is its foundation.'

ÓDouwe reached into the middle of his labyrinth, pulled his cup to him and emptied it into his throat. A discoloured fog hung about his head.

'Are you going to intervene on my behalf?' Craebeckx asked him. 'Speak for me against the criminal Zijss?'

'Yes, yes, intervene…' ÓDouwe noticed that the old man's ears protruded comically, with the setting sun warming up the blood in them. 'Your life story isn't all that's in there, is it?'

'We discussed many things besides. I told him to record it all.'

'Now Judith, she's friends with those cockless swots – I mean those doctors, especially Norvell, your former secretary, whose plan is to convert the Jews to Christianity.' (Culo creaked in his chair.)

'Would that be such a bad thing?' said Craebeckx.

ÓDouwe managed a bleak little laugh. 'What exactly do you think we have Jews for in the first place? For our amusement?'

Craebeckx struggled again with his ageing dignity.

'Are you engaged in a secret war with your daughter over this? That's what I really want to know. Or anyone with his daughter? Is this the kind of thing that goes on all the time without me noticing?' ÓDouwe was staring at him, perhaps wanting an answer. When none came, he picked up the book. 'John Norvell and his cronics – and you, no not you – have developed the completely crazy, or perhaps reasonably sound, idea that the preparation for the thousand years of Christ's reign here on Earth must include the conversion of the Jews to the True Faith. Once accomplished – perhaps there are other steps they must take as well – we'll have our thousand years, followed by the Last Day when the final accounts will be reckoned. You see? Is that a prospect you would relish? Not I. And I think I make no special case. I think it's a general case.'

'These are John's ideas, not mine. And you think that by stopping these people from their course you can delay the final Judgement of

God?' Craebeckx widened his eyes to gather in the full picture.

'Delay God?' ÓDouwe lost himself for a moment in the idea. 'And so those who would oppose the converters might fare better in this immediate stretch of life.'

Unexpectedly, Culo's voice drifted across the darkness. 'What's old Jesus going to say to you when you go meet him, Mr ÓDouwe?' He audibly licked a tooth, feeling the full moon of the policeman's face orienting towards him.

Craebeckx hurried on, edging behind ÓDouwe's argument, 'So you're saying that I'm your ally by serving the cause of the Jews against these others?'

'Oh, but then you would be an enemy of that which is. Is now. You see the trouble even at the gates of the labyrinth. Even before we have chosen our door and boldly made our beginning.'

'You should know better than any that a Mennonite shuns politics,' said Craebeckx.

'I certainly should know it, for that is what Mennonites have repeatedly told me. But all it means to me is that you think the office which I serve is shit.' He laid his palm on the book as if about to swear an oath. 'The elusive Zijss, the Bankruptcy Court, peat mismanagement – I see you'll have no peat in your house – your treacherous Counsel, your dubious secretary Norvell, his mystical friends, Catholics, Mennonites, Jews…' He refilled his cup, took another mouthful. 'A counterfeit Pekelharing, your daughter at the moth-house, your man called Arse,' (He paused for any reaction from Culo, but none came), 'the cloven hoof of the Apocalypse, the end of the world, the end of the States, treason therefore, your foreign adventures, the Spanish, the Portuguese, the South, the unholy family van Bosvelt, more unspeakable acts, who knows what devilry, or trickery…' He puffed several times at his pipe. Thin streams of smoke wound past his ear. 'You know how far I've been? Out of all the whole world? Amsterdam. That's the furthest. The Big City. Nowhere foreign. Not even down south. What do you think about that?'

'Not even Ireland?'

ÓDouwe glared for a moment, but seemed to lack the strength to sustain the necessary mood. 'Perhaps we are all faded monarchs delivered against our will into strange realms. Has ten Brink been coming round here, by the way?'

'Who?'

'Who, indeed. My fucking sergeant. Where is he now, for instance? Off on some secret mission of his own. He has me watched, you know.'

'Why don't you get rid of him?'

'He's already ingratiated himself upstairs, made himself necessary. Could have him killed, I suppose.'

'Do you want to add another fatal sin to the catalogue?' said Craebeckx.

'Must be all that gloomjuice he's so fond of,' added Culo in a low voice.

○

As Mrs van Bosvelt ascended the staircase, ÓDouwe was prickling at the danger, having already planned his response in the event of her trying something again, but careful all the while not to provoke her. She was with Lennep, talking to him – never a good sign.

'What are you doing up here?' ÓDouwe said to Lennep.

'Sorry sir, I told her, but she said you said I should come up.'

'Well I didn't.'

'Shall I go back down again?'

Judith stood in the far doorway. Mrs van Bosvelt addressed her in a quiet, steady, sane tone. 'I just want to see her. May I?'

ÓDouwe wondered at her first fetching Lennep – a wily message of persuasion, showing him she would go under guard. But madness has its tranquil possessings too.

Agatha's face appeared behind Judith's, and due to their different statures, above it also. Momentarily, the doorway framed a two-headed creature, made of two types of beauty, or a woeful blend related to the Gorgon: they were instantly an outward apparition of Mrs van Bosvelt's inner state, but without solving its central question. ÓDouwe's hand moved towards his glass.

'Madam my Mother…' Agatha began.

'You've put on weight,' said her mother.

Agatha looked down at herself, wondering at changes in general. 'Thank you.'

'Have you done something to your hair?'

'No, I don't think so. It's grown a little.'

'You're so pretty now, so grown up.' These ordinary exchanges, laced with their charge of conditional approval, tended to lull everyone. And now Mrs van Bosvelt walked towards the doorway. Lennep quickly checked with ÓDouwe who stood up, nodded at him and stepped forward a pace or two.

Agatha's mother entered the place that had been barred to her for some weeks. Lennep followed. ÓDouwe moved across the hallway after them. Oopjen was standing to attention, hanging her head, hoping to be ignored. Mrs van Bosvelt was taking in the new arrangements, the extra sleeping-closets, all the other siege furnishings. Having completed her survey, smiling now, she approached her daughter whilst withdrawing her knife.

Lennep's attention had slid out of focus. It had been a while since he had been this close to Agatha. Responding first to ÓDouwe's yell, therefore, rather than the sight of the weapon, he recovered quickly, bounded forward and swung his fist squarely and heavily into Mrs van

Bosvelt's face and she fell like a slaughtered animal. ÓDouwe was close behind and pushed him out of the way.

The other women shrieked.

ÓDouwe picked up the knife. 'Quiet!' His forehead was glistening. He was searching for plausible excuses for himself. 'Fuck it!' It had already occurred to him that Agatha's death might be the solution to her life. If Lennep had been slower, the whole thing might have been nicely cleared up. But if Lennep hadn't been there at all, might ÓDouwe himself have held back? God knows his reflexes weren't what they used to be. 'She pay you?' he said to Lennep with extraordinary venom.

Lennep recoiled, surprised, his eye on the knife gripped tight in his master's hand.

Agatha collapsed.

'She's hurt!' said Judith. 'Help her!'

ÓDouwe used the knife to cut open Agatha's dress. Oopjen shrieked again. The wound was to her shoulder, deep, to the bone, oozing blood. Apt, he thought, that the creature who gave birth to the aberration would also be the agent of her death.

But he couldn't let her die now: if she died, he'd have to kill them all. He looked from face to face. He'd have to start with Lennep, then do Judith, then the maid… He put the knife in his belt and flicked his fingers at Oopjen. 'Bring me something, a rag, anything.' And then to Lennep he said, 'Go and get the other two.'

To Lennep's tuned ear, this smacked of demotion or danger. 'I don't know where they are, sir.'

ÓDouwe gave him a poisonous look. 'Neither do I. Try my house. Or Norvell's.' Lennep waited while ÓDouwe was still visibly thinking. 'Or Mrs Bleckker's.'

When he had gone, ÓDouwe lifted Agatha onto the bed, told Judith to press the cloth hard to the wound and had Oopjen fetch the surgeon.

‘And the physician, sir?’ she said to him timidly.

ÓDouwe was uncomprehending.

‘Madam always has both, sir.’

‘Alright, but be quick!’

While they were busy with Agatha, he grabbed the unconscious Mrs van Bosvelt by the arms and dragged her body across the passageway into his own room where he propped her against the wall out of their line of sight, bound her hands and feet, pulled his chair up and settled in with pipe and flask, waiting for his breathing to slow down.

On waking, Mrs van Bosvelt immediately complained of the pain in her head and face. Then when she found she couldn’t raise her hand to those tender parts, she complained of being tied up.

‘Quiet down or I’ll bring him in here for another crack at your vile face.’

She lapped at the blood on her lip and winced at the pain. ‘Where’s my daughter?’

‘Which one?’

This silenced her for a moment, then she said, ‘What shall we do now?’

‘Wait.’ ÓDouwe refreshed his drink.

Mrs van Bosvelt eyed it thirstily. ‘I think I forgot to eat today.’

‘Why?’

He became conscious of a prolonged examination. ‘People have to wear uniforms,’ she said at last, ‘or nothing gets done.’

‘Is that so remarkable?’

‘Is that part of your uniform now?’ She nodded towards his bottle.

ÓDouwe had been swinging around to the opinion – laced with its hint of sham, he knew – that if the delicate business of Justice were to achieve anything, it must feed back into its equation the qualities of the dispenser of it. Without men like himself (in other words), without those subtleties of character and, indeed, appetites… Men of will, with their peculiar leanings towards certain categories of order… He chased the last two drops out of the bottom of the glass and made a sour face as he refilled it. 'The miser, the misanthrope, the hypocrite – that's me. And don't make the mistake of thinking that these aren't the highest of human values.'

Mrs van Bosvelt watched him cautiously.

ÓDouwe began to sing quietly, his eyes all aglitter, his hands frisky in the air. 'I'm so in love, and I've got a dead body walking about in the next room. She's all pretty and pink just as if she weren't dead. Let's not bury her like decent Christians. Let's have her walk about the place as if she didn't infect the whole city with her filthy stench that everyone pretends they can't smell!' (Pronounced, 'Ssssuhmellllllaagh!) The last part of his song, being so long a sentence, consumed all his breath and made him red in the cheeks.

Mrs van Bosvelt wiped her bloody mouth on her shoulder in an awkward movement. 'We're all your prisoners. Hostages. Shouldn't you be demanding a ransom from someone?'

He lowered his hands and used them to fix himself another drink. Her madness, assuaged by her bonds (he supposed), might be a good place to deposit his own madness – a strategy forming inside a cloud in the manner of dramatic weather. 'Everything trips along in one way for thousands of years,' he said, 'and then something else, some new element, some novel trick is introduced. It's a joke. We're meant to laugh. But then it's not funny. Nobody on the face of this Earth finds it funny. So it's not a joke. It's a lesson. I know, I'll just kill a child, and when you think the full extent of the harm has been reached, I'll drop her straight back into your laps. Or I'll replace her, perhaps with her twin, the one no-one's ever heard of or seen before…'

'You're like me.' Her face was richly spiteful.

'How am I like you? You're insane. You seem alright now, but don't you remember what you did just now, you devil? Or yesterday? And what will you do tomorrow when you're conveniently out of your wits again?'

Mrs van Bosvelt, her lips tightly closed, subjected the policeman to another lengthy examination. 'The devil is a viceroy,' she said finally.

Setting tributes on false altars might well be his fate. Employed in the service of the darkness which serves the light. An unhappy career, and an excuse if ever there was one – certainly an improvement on his current sorry collection of excuses.

Lennep, Backer and Meer had arrived and were horsing about at the foot of the stairs. ÓDouwe called them up. They took in the scene of the bleeding and bound woman, and their master stretched out on his chair with a bottle in his lap. Mrs van Bosvelt hissed quietly in their direction.

'Gag her,' ÓDouwe said.

○

Maria touched ÓDouwe's elbow lightly. All being upside down and backwards and some of it probably not well with God, and Mr ÓDouwe sinking into his cup, she did this in case simplicity and ease return to him (or mighty powers be transferred to herself).

For his part, an interlude of mental humming instead of any direct thought of Agatha's various paradoxical states. But once disturbed, he turned on Maria swiftly. 'Just whatever's on top!' He was referring to her imminent trip to the cellar on his behalf.

Agatha's breathing was slow and shallow. She looked as she had previously when he had examined her post-mortem. He lowered his face close to hers in order to feel her breath on his lips.

The physician and the surgeon, both damp from the unceasing rains, continued their watchfulness of ÓDouwe for a few more moments before returning to each other, whispering sharply. In former times for medical emergencies, Mrs van Bosvelt would have them summoned together as a matter of caution or superfluous wealth or wicked caprice.

'Be warned,' said the surgeon, 'If she's not bled properly, she'll decline. Is that what you want?'

'Being dense,' the physician hissed under his cone, 'you wouldn't have noticed that the Great Lady only has you here to cause pain to me for her own high amusement. I accept that pain – on her account, not yours. Otherwise why do you suppose your methods have not been used?'

'Because you stopped me. It's you she keeps to provoke me. You serve no other purpose. Man is more interesting to you in death than in life, you ghoul.'

'I act on Madam's wishes. Could she physically restrain you? No, so I must.' The physician wondered vaguely whether Mrs van Bosvelt might be nearby to corroborate his claim.

'Blind force is the whole of your authority,' said the surgeon.

'I have dissected, therefore I have knowledge. Blood flows within, doing good to life. You have peered into the scrying glass and kissed the devil's arse.'

'I have diagnosed—'

'Diagnosed what? That she has been slashed with a big knife? Bravo!'

'The underlying causes.'

'And what's the underlying cause for completely useless ignorance?'

'Graverobber.'

'Bloodsucker.'

'Necromancer.'

'Satanist.'

'Arsehole.'

'Cunt.'

'Ooh good, is there going to be a fight?' ÓDouwe was smiling and rubbing his palms together. 'Shall she live, then?' he added.

'If God wills it so,' answered the physician, bowing slightly at the thought.

'Christ,' replied the policeman. A flicker in the far corner indicated some rumpled discontinuity of the wall which startled him. 'Judith?' he said, clutching his empty glass, wondering. She had entered discreetly. She came forward, bent towards the patient and spoke quietly to her. ÓDouwe secretly watched the moving lips in profile.

Maria returned rattling her tray. 'Pour,' said ÓDouwe.

A groan issued from the bed. The medics leaned in. ÓDouwe emptied his glass and held it out to be refilled.

'Is that the first she's spoken?' asked Judith.

'She spoke earlier,' replied the physician, 'She was merely sleeping just now.'

ÓDouwe laid down his glass and smoothed a crease in the bedcover with his black glove. Everyone's attention went to the trespassing hand. It reached over to one of Agatha's and picked it up. It hung inert in his, but her eyes were on him. 'And what did she say?' asked ÓDouwe.

'She asked why everything is grey.'

'Is that normal?'

The medics exchanged a glance and shrugged.

Judith began caressing Agatha's brow and murmuring softly to her. ÓDouwe put his head between theirs and said quietly to Agatha. 'Where have you been?'

It took Agatha a while to summon the air to her throat. 'Been?' she croaked. 'I don't know.'

Close up, the policeman's face lacked blood, except where it clung on in the fine colonies of veins on his cheeks and nose. Its sweaty surface glistened under the force of a continual tremor. Agatha had merely lost a lot of blood in the attack, but to a fevered mind she might seem to be engaged in a pact with her former state. 'Where have you been, Agnes, so close to death?' ÓDouwe was whispering to the patient again. 'It's you your Mother wanted all along, not the other girl.'

'Who's Agnes?' Agatha asked in a weak voice.

'If you could see yourself now. Your mad Mother floats towards you, and you repel her. Why?'

She tried to turn away.

'She goes to you, you who are elsewhere. She doesn't know what she's doing. She's simple, for all her money.'

'I'm here,' said Agatha, beginning to be alarmed in the quivery way of the infirm.

'But look at you!' ÓDouwe's eyes seemed to vibrate gently. 'I'm looking at you now, but you're elsewhere. Where are you? You're another person.'

'I'm Agatha,' she cried hoarsely, trying to raise herself from the bed.

Judith elbowed forward and eased her down again. 'Let her rest.'

'Agatha? That's just a word,' said ÓDouwe, ignoring Judith, trying to dodge his head back into the gap between them. 'Your Mother wanted to find you, but you evaded her. You're her sentinel, one cadaver over another. Do you hate her so much? That you would reverse your birth?'

'You're drunk,' protested Agatha, shutting her eyes, while Judith stroked her hair.

'No, that's not it.'

The medics straightened up. 'What's that noise?' asked the surgeon.

'Christ!' ÓDouwe went to the window and called down. 'I told you to do it somewhere else!'

'Sorry sir.' Backer and Meer were standing over Lennep who was sprawled on the ground holding up an arm to protect himself from their blows. 'But you told us to surprise him, sir,' said Backer. They held their cudgels mid-swing. 'When we got here, he thought he was in the clear, sir,' added Meer, laughing at his comrade's folly.

‘Alright. Hurry up.’

Lennep whimpered.

‘Yes sir!’ said Backer as the two of them again bent over Lennep and applied their cudgels to the softer parts of his body while he yelped and twisted. When they were satisfied with their work, Backer reached into Lennep’s pocket and removed his purse loaded with gold. Meer waited for Backer’s sign, then took out his knife and pressed it to Lennep’s cheek, drawing along it a thin line of blood, while Lennep bawled like a disappointed child.

‘What is it?’ insisted the physician.

‘That’ll be my men,’ ÓDouwe replied dryly, pulling his head back in. ‘Doing their work.’

○

John Norvell was at his habitual post, looking out. Gerrit van Oelst was standing behind him, some way off, with his back to him. This arrangement, simple though it might seem, was barnacled all about its hull with evidence of travail: only one of them wanted something from the other, but it wasn’t possible for either to decide which was the supplicant and which the benefactor. Each frowned into this matt black mirror in a state of suspended hope until John urged into Gerrit’s damp hands a heavy-looking tight roll of paper. Gerrit’s gloved fingers fiddled at one of the knots on the haphazard net of twine that bound it while John followed up with a knife, blade forward, eyes wide and keen.

These preliminaries over, acute shapes of terror and anguish slinking out of sight, Gerrit peered at the inscrutable rune on the first leaf and flicked over to the next page. He moved in close to the window and tilted it away from his dripping hat the better to see the spider tracks, buckety loops and reckless veerings towards the paper’s precipitous edge. 'The kermis', he began reading, and encouraged by John showing the highlight on one of his teeth, he continued: 'is nonsense bubbling up from the past. Like a hot spring in a sulphuric marsh, the bubbles rise through other bubbles which themselves have been given life from older ones, and remain for a time, standing proud of the surface, formed of warm gloop.'

There he paused for confirmation that John was appreciative of his reading style, his arm still in the air. John was more attentive to the arm than the style, to its convex musculature which presented vivid contrast with the pale wilted bone fixed at his own side. He repeated the word 'gloop' which Gerrit took as his cue to go on: 'Any fool can easily trace the modern seven-day piss-festival of the kermis back a mere generation or so to the kirk mass dedication of a new church, which itself is the States' version of the Catholic version of the Jewish dedication of the Altar, otherwise known to those people as Hanukkah. And there you have it: God made the world, and here we are in it thinking these sober thoughts.'

Here Gerrit paused to gently tap his teeth together – a minor, a symbolic, gnashing.

'You're thinking something's a bit wrong. You're thinking the sum—. You're thinking—' Surfacing consciousness of interlude, some distraction of delayed time, one of those long-legged flies wafting news impossible to translate.

Taken with his own performance, Gerrit pressed on. 'But no, there's trouble afoot and, unusually, it has nothing to do with Catholics or Jews. Hanukkah, merely by chance, coincides with the celebrations of the shortest day of the year, Helios's birthday, and the feasts of Dionysos. Dionysos, that is, who loved Carya, whose name derives from the bee, Ker. She was a Laconian princess whose corpse Dionysos transformed into a walnut tree which the Laconian women subsequently danced around in annual ceremony. Think now of the kermis tree gaily circumnavigated for no good reason by our own red-cheeked virgins.'

Gerrit caught John quietly reciting the last few words with him and used this hiatus to mentally direct the virgins the other way around their tree.

John's lips closed and Gerrit quickly read on. 'The bee-goddess Ker, the ancient deity of Fate, was served by the Keres whose job it was to cruelly destroy those whose time had come to be delivered to the shadows. And here in the centre of our historical labyrinth, a light is shone on the actual character of that yearly festival as it is experienced by the people of the Virgin City and our neighbours who come to share in it: it is a ragged expression of our knowledge of the tenuous suspension of our fate. Look at the extremity brought to bear on the matter, the parade of nature's freaks, the mortal excess, the crazy and often useless invention. All of life is crammed in, and more, a concentration of life. This is our yearly desperate bargain with fate to suspend the blow and ease the punishment, our case being that life and our earthly endeavours are worth the trouble. Plainly, this is a Pagan and not a Christian bargain.'

'What I'm saying—' But John couldn't say. He returned to the comfort of his window.

'One might almost say' (Gerrit continued) 'that the dedication of Christian churches is merely a weak interruption to the progress of an ancient spirit. No wonder the doctors don't like it very much, though their reasons are always to do with the Catholic connection, or with the licentiousness of it, which amounts to the same thing.'

'Same thing,' John repeated.

'However,' (Gerrit read on) 'if these speculations give offence, think only that at the time of the kermis, licence is given for all sorts of things, including thoughts such as these.'

Gerrit's eye drifted past John towards the window where the never-ending rains slanted down. Us. Us. (He was no longer reading, but thinking.) Something in that word, that idea, struck him with special force. Some dimension of meaning was sliding towards him framed in pale light. Us! But then it was gone. 'It's not madness. Or not *just* madness. That's what you're saying?'

Agatha's headless corpse was found in the woods. Three days later it walked back into town without the slightest hint of irony. The investigation into her death descended the scale of rationality to... rationale, ration, ratio. So why be surprised if Mr ÓDouwe wanted to peer into the murky workings of the painters? Us.

ÓDouwe's latest trick was to rave about the two Pekelharings that this year's kermis had produced. Little comfort to Gerrit that ÓDouwe didn't know that the second, counterfeit, Pekelharing had been Gerrit himself. Sooner or later ÓDouwe might well discover this fact and – miserable prospect – apply his inquisitive method to Gerrit over it. These days, ÓDouwe was like one of those square-faced dogs clamping on with iron jaw, impossible to shake off or even get any kind of a decent hold of. His was the authority of an animal bred to single purpose, oblivious of counter-argument.

Back then at a certain moment of that long kermis, the official Pekelharing had been pretending to want to eat an apple while failing to decide where to make a start on it, and he was doing this in front of a man, his chosen victim of the moment, who had been heartily consuming a similar fruit until presented with this bent mirror of himself. The man was unsure whether to be amused or insulted, whether escape would reflect well or badly on him, whether to crystallise these mixed responses into anger or humility, opposition or collusion. So now there were two types of hesitancy in intimate conversation with each other, bound by the laughter of passers-by.

This was the unfortunate moment for the appearance of the second

Pekelharing (Gerrit) producing in the first one new refinements of indecision: the authentic Pekelharing froze mid-gesture. He was angry. He was suspicious. He was sad. Quick as you like though, he assimilated these feelings into fuel for his game. He ignored the impostor and returned his full attention to his current victim, drew the apple slowly, slowly towards his face, all the while immobilising his victim with an unblinking gaze of terrifying authority, and slowly, slowly bit into the apple, tore off a piece with his teeth and began chewing. When he looked down at the apple, turning it thoughtfully in his hand, chewing all the while, the victim recognised it as his cue to go.

Pekelharing swallowed, and deftly launched the remains of the apple in a high arc over his head. It dropped into the canal a few yards behind him, threw up a coronet of murky water and bobbed on its surface.

Now he was ready for Gerrit. He seemed to float towards him borne an inch above the surface of the road. How had he achieved this trick? Gerrit looked back at the scene in his memory. Beneath the makeup, the clown's eyes expressed… absence of fear, so thoroughly that they also brimmed with rich potentialities of amusement and compassion. The rest of the body followed the will of the eyes, was its extraneous organ, was formed of its harmonies, therefore did their bidding smoothly. He was a clown of the eyes. Gerrit saw the meaning of the costume, too, in terms of those eyes, saw the adornment, its excess, its folly, its pleasure in its futility, its wayward ruching, its ribbons, pleats and frills extravagant in their lack of sense.

Gerrit was becoming exceedingly conscious of the difference between the two versions of Pekelharing. The real one was also a man for sure, though not known personally to Gerrit, a man of the playhouse, the fair, the tavern, the road, the night, and on the occasion in question, the scandalous daylight. Gerrit clung as to a hunk of flotsam to the idea that his own addled imposture was by its own lights an exercise in the rigours of foolery, but he knew this lie was perfectly transparent to the real Pekelharing. He had one other refuge, learned so recently from the clown's last victim, to synthesise the manifold tensions straining one against another into a concerted attitude of resistance. He braced himself. Pekelharing was half an arm's length from him, facing him squarely, bending slightly at the knees, flexing gently on that support he made for himself of his own legs (the man has just invented his own legs! thought Gerrit, but with some relief that such expertise was likely to require minimal bile in its service). Pekelharing dangled his arms loosely from his shoulders, in imitation of the ape? the hanged man? No, he was a man retiring his arms, surplus tools, from present duty. He stuck out his lower lip. His eyes were prodigiously calm. Gerrit tried a variety of responses: a grimace, a frown, a humid smile – the full repertoire of the corpse twisting in the wind, not yet quite dead.

What had got into him dressing up like this and besporting himself at large? Party spirit on its own would be no good as an excuse. Memory true or false told him that he had thought to modify the Pekelharing act in favour of something more genuinely absurd, deaf to reason, shapeless – to produce a clown with no insight. Mid-life worries might be included in the account: a single man, a late man, not high in his profession, teaching privileged children things they were not keen to learn. In such frames of mind, a coup is often indicated. His own kermis then, with himself no longer a body in a herd. The other option, favoured by many a bypassed spirit: to hide indoors, fingers in ears, perhaps drowning the shrill debauch with prayer, still mindful to quell even his own enthusiasm in matters pious.

So for Gerrit, two purposes, or is that three? And two (three?) directions. The net result would bear this out with Gerrit placing himself directly in the path of the juggernaut, head bowed for absolution or doom.

Which doom was delivered by Pekelharing in the form of a minor shift in the focus of those eyes of his, so that it appeared that Gerrit was no longer visible to him, no longer counted, and when Pekelharing was satisfied his work was done – a matter of a few seconds – he moved off.

Gerrit moved off too and saw Agatha nearby, buffered either side by her maids. Had she seen him, she may not have even recognised him – he, disguise apart, having been rendered insubstantial. Probably she hadn't or ÓDouwe, who Gerrit knew was searching for this second mysterious clown, would have prised it out of her by now.

Gerrit's long silence got John's attention. The painter was thinking of using the notebook to fan the gross odours of the room away from his face. 'I heard they arrested that clown,' said Gerrit. The notebook had taken on a new shape in his hand – that of a thing already in flight across a void, momentarily weightless but loaded with inertial drag.

'Did they?' John made an odd face expressing a bundle of tiny emotions, experimentally clownish, suddenly adept.

'Hasn't ÓDouwe said anything to you?'

In his persona as the left hand of the Law, John became alert and evasive. 'Me? No. Why should he? He has several times mentioned that camera picture of yours, though. What it was… how it worked… I told him I was in the dark same as him.' Gerrit moved his hand in some unconscious gesture of defence that rattled the notebook. John was moved to blend complex notes of warning and irresponsibility: 'He wasn't happy.'

'He came to me looking for it.' Gerrit was conscious of conveying a message to ÓDouwe through this version of John. 'I told him it had faded away. Showed him. He went crazy, wanted to know why I'd destroyed evidence.' Gerrit looked past John to the window again. 'Can you see him now?'

John moved. 'Wait. Yes.'

'What's he doing?'

'Smoking. Drinking. Talking to Judith.'

○

'You are small.' Having said this, ÓDouwe turned his face to the fire to let Judith examine him at her leisure. He meant to give nothing away – nothing in the line of respite, that is.

She looked where he looked. The glowing fissurcs in the peat seemed like an illusion: volcanic, antediluvian, prelapsarian even, and therefore senseless and terrifying – or a little vision, both near and far, of that place where demons, as they say, do God's other work.

She looked sideways, saw that something had ratcheted forward in him. The sweat-greased face and the never-still hands were by now familiar. But even in this state he was busy conjuring some trick or other. Her sly answer was to offer him another drink.

He considered whether she had just now seen the wrong things in him, given that he had taken to improving these performances in front of the mirror. Was she laughing at him? The answer was refracted half a dozen ways through overheated mental plasmas. He thought of manfully declining the offer just to show her, and to bolster such boldness he'd need a drink or two. Catching himself, he turned the question over again. She had arranged herself like a little statue of a servant, obediently attending the master, safe behind a screen of pure mockery. He saw through her game and felt the rush of optimism one gets just before sinking the first celebratory glass of the evening. Again he caught the snake coiling around its own body. Judith had barely blinked since the first temptation, the first test. Exhausted, he reasoned that his character and achievements were securely fixed in the great account no matter what happened from now on. Just the one, then, to fortify the depleted spirit… He showed her who was in charge by ostentatiously gulping the whole lot down and exhaling appreciatively through a wide open mouth. While she refilled, he tweaked his victory, twisting various wild strands to form a single rope. 'There's no getting away from this important fact. Smallness of stature is an established mark of wickedness.'

She said, 'I thought you knew better than that, but you don't.'

Stature might well be the index of an evil heart that otherwise conceals itself, ÓDouwe thought. We should trust the inner voice on these matters, as well as the Law. She is altogether improbable. How to voice such a notion? New filaments of reason bind and strengthen. An eggshell enclosing putrefaction?

His face-shifting began to alarm her.

Judith had this way with her and he was wise to it: at any point in any conversation, she reserved the right to fall silent. It was supposed to reflect onto the questioner the folly of his pursuit. It was supposed to force him to track backwards to the decisions that brought him to this point, all the way back to that first many-forked junction and make him choose again. Well, the trick used to work when it was new to him, but not now. He had steadily cultivated his own silence – but of course the meaning of her silences could only be outdone by a greater moral weight. That was the trick of it, perhaps attainable in these extraordinary circumstances. 'Agatha is small too, but not as small as you, therefore the lesser of the two in wickedness.'

'Imagine, Mr ÓDouwe, an objective observer, a philosopher—'

'Like John Norvell, you mean?'

'Any philosopher, having to choose between the two of us which one is possessed of any number of evils including intoxication by liquor, by anger, by disappointment, by hatred and by self-pity. And then there's murder…'

'What murder?'

'Where is Agatha's Mother? No answer. You're right to look down.

Down is the correct destination.'

'The Mother is safe. I don't know about the daughter. The daughter is the question.'

'The Mother was your prisoner. Now dead, I hear.'

'She has gone among the bee-worshippers to do who knows what further harm.'

'The what?' The mechanism was creaking audibly. Judith waited for the click of another notch.

'We had our own festival, you know.' He absently held his glass up to the light. 'We had a goat on a bier, alive mind you, tethered, garlanded.' Click. 'We fed it the first crop of ale. It was carried shoulder high around the town like a god and we his acolytes. The whole thing lasted four whole days and nights. You think the kermis extreme. A parade of sober judges by comparison. Nothing I've seen before or since can compare to a Kerryman in drink.'

'Kerry? That's where you're from?'

'Did I say Kerry? I meant Derry. That, I think you'll find, will explain Mr Roel ten Brink's attitude. He has no time for anyone outside of our City. He's even suspicious of anyone born on the far side of the perimeter wall. I, mere footsoldier, got this job, you see, not just through bribery, but because they needed someone to absolve them of their sins. As far as they're concerned, I'm a sort of Jew, tolerated in order to break Christian Law on their behalf. Whereas in fact I'm royalty.'

Creak, click. 'What about Mrs van Bosvelt?'

'I'm telling you. The old Irish kings presiding over poets and sages – you lot, in other words. The last recognised in that line, I might tell you, was one Fearghal mac Maoile Duin. And as far as I'm concerned, that line like any other only seemed to be broken. Of course, there's been no break between a thousand years ago and today. Everything continues one way or another.'

'You've broken the family van Bosvelt? It continues in some other form, one way or another? I'm to blame for one, you're not to blame for the other? This is what you're saying? I'm a witch and you're a king?'

'Unless you can come up with something better.'

○

A rustling made John turn from his telescope. He had been watching Gerrit repeatedly pushing towards the ceiling an open-topped box full of rabbits, over the rim of which white tails and pink noses twitched, while all around, many kittens showed a keen interest.

ÓDouwe was fanning his own nose with a ragged bundle of papers tied with string.

'Are those my notebooks? Are they all there?' John looked dubiously at the untidy package.

'You might open a window.' The policeman smiled. 'Ten Brink's been here. I can smell him.'

'You can?'

'What did he want? Did he announce himself in advance, or was his visit a complete surprise to you?'

'He was here briefly. He did as you're doing now. He stood to one side of the window not wanting to be seen, keeping watch. He took money from me.'

'What for? What for?'

'He wants me to keep him informed about – and this is what he said exactly – everything I see, everything I hear, everything I hear about, and everything I think about it.'

'What information have you given him so far? What have you told him about me?'

'Nothing. I don't know anything. What should I tell him?'

'Say I collected my payment from you.' He came closer, eyes pink, hair streaked against forehead, nose averted, gloved hand outstretched. John found his purse and counted out seven coins. ÓDouwe frowned at them, swayed on his feet, and closed his fist. John waited nervously. The policeman remembered the papers in his other hand. 'Very occasionally, but only when I feel like it, I obey God.'

John followed the horsefly orbit of his papers. The bindings had been torn apart and some pages had come loose from under the string and were falling on the floor.

'Agatha, her Mother, John Norvell.' ÓDouwe had cranked up again, waving the papers for emphasis at John's face. 'Judith Craebeckx, old Craebeckx, that bloody Culo, Zijss of course, always Zijss, relatives here, there and everywhere, Judith and John,' – jab, wave – 'that idiot Gerrit van Oelst, that little bastard Cornelis ter Gouw, ten Brink, ten Brink, where doth he slink? And John with his ink, and corpses that stink...' ÓDouwe looked at the coins in his hand as if they were objects of unknown meaning before dropping them into a pocket. 'Signs, signs,' he went on, after which there was a long silence while his body teetered on its faulty axis. 'You know how I see it? I see it like a door. Shall we open it? Everyone's talking about opening it or not opening it. I've got a feeling we shouldn't.'

John's own mind was edging towards thoughts of escape.

'Here, these are yours, I think.' ÓDouwe tossed the thick bundle of papers onto the table. More of the pages fluttered to the ground. 'Everything is as it should be, as regards my office, my duties. Which are, as we all know, mysterious.'

'You've had it all translated, then? So you know it's all nothing.'

The skin around ÓDouwe's eyes was yellow and dry like old paper. '*He reveals the deep and secret things: He knows what is in the darkness.* Don't be surprised. In a way, though mere footsoldier, I aspire to God's point of view.' He trailed off again looking gravely sad.

Thinking of Judith, John said, 'It's not true that you had that gypsy boy Paul Janse crucified, the one who couldn't talk, is it?'

ÓDouwe shook his head. Is that what we're here for? Perhaps it is, after all. 'There are fifty hanging corpses on the roads leading out from here in every direction,' he said using a professional tone. 'Do you expect me to check them all?' The sand-clock hissed gently. 'Well, I suppose a lot of foolish things happen in a life. If you laid them end to end, they'd probably circle the globe many times over.' He took three steps, turned, a futile journey. 'The end of the world?' He pointed at the bundle of notebooks. 'You keep going on about the end of the world. But it's happened already!'

○

Pekelharing in his ragged and filthy costume waited for his interrogator to speak. His body shivered, ached, hungered, wanted sleep. He let the random visions to which he was host come and go. Each tremor was a sign of approaching death which was his ally against the loveless hardships of his present world. He had only one piece of work to accomplish, and that at all times – to let fall what may. What was falling now was ÓDouwe in his comfortable chair behind his big table. On it were the papers relating to his state. The papers said nothing; his state was nothing. Beside these were his jug and cup, also relating to his state. Pekelharing considered his own thirst, considered how want of water occupied his mind, how the mind itself mistakenly seemed to want water.

The insult to life that gathered itself behind that desk, the brazen challenge to beauty and intelligence, the imposition of its weight to the exclusion of all else, its demand for continual recognition, this too was a portion of the opposing reality that must be let fall where it may and

spend its vicious energies without Pekelharing's help.

But between drinks, and even during drinks, ÓDouwe had an inkling of all this too, so he kept quiet with a view to causing the clown much inconvenience. Also, had they not already talked on several occasions? Greater hardship than the clown now suffered was not yet in ÓDouwe's plan. He so heartily wished for a voluntary, worldly, correspondence between the two of them. Confessions wrung from prisoners lacked that nice gossipy note of conspiracy – evidential in itself, especially in matters so dramatically of the spheres.

So Pekelharing – whose real name turned out to be Roel van den Vondel, the Christian name a minor coincidence that caused ÓDouwe to measure its potential for dangerous significance – shivered in silence.

Matters for consideration: What are clowns? Are they funny? Stupid? Are they magicians of some sort? (Could this one make pictures appear out of nowhere, untouched by human hand, for example?) Do they mock us with their whimsy? And if so, by what right? Am *I* mocked?

Two Pekelharings at war with each other (with corresponding legions raging in the ether), two selves, and who saw them? Why, it was Agatha. So what did she really see? Or should that be two Agathas seeing two Pekelharings, one each. Therefore one or other of these incidents didn't happen: one of each or two of each, not one of one and two of the other. If two, which Pekelharing would this be? The one seen by Agatha or the one seen by Agnes?

The sand-clock had long since ceased its hissing, and ÓDouwe thought about resetting it, thought about the effect resetting it might produce: might he seem impatient, frivolous, anxious – cruel? Sound-effects were otherwise provided by the rain lashing at the window. Reminiscent of lost pleasures, it impacted in infinite variety of pattern, through which mobile blurs of trees and houses shimmered. It interested Pekelharing, whose windowless cell was ill-lit by a gap high in the wall giving onto a corridor, itself ill-lit by a small lamp.

○

While Agatha, captive in her bed, convalesced, ÓDouwe had many opportunities to deteriorate in front of her. Just now, all he wanted to do was gaze blearily at her through the bottom of his glass. Turning, she was caught unawares and let out a quick scream, weak and hoarse, which caused a twinge in her wound. He pulled back and calmed her with an outstretched hand. Like it or not, he had pressing business. Of late, he was following up the 'clue' of the camera picture and its bearing on this most difficult of all cases. He had Gerrit van Oelst and John Norvell in to question her from a technical point of view about the thing which they could not entirely explain with their Arabian science. They were standing behind him now, waiting for his signal. Independently of the policeman, they had surmised quite reasonably that the missing element was artfully black, and naturally they were willing to come a-calling to see if the creature would reveal her connection to it, whether that be accidental or deliberate.

All three of them gazed at her wide-eyed as if they really thought she would spill the beans. Ons meanwhile looked down upon them all from her high perch, undisturbed, curious and, within her range, thoughtful. Likewise, Judith held herself apart even though she too wondered at Agatha's connection to the camera picture, and she told herself that the percentage of witchery she might attribute to Agatha as the decisive catalyst was significantly less than the percentage the men attributed to her. In this way, Judith put herself morally ahead of them.

From time to time Oopjen, sensing error in all of this, uttered prayers under her breath.

When ÓDouwe was ready to give the signal, John hung back, in awe of Agatha's beauty perhaps, which was refined by her feeble condition, and conscious for once of the high contrast of his own condition. He tapped van Oelst on his back and whispered, 'Ask her about *eau prime*.'

Gerrit was relieved that this present fuss was not about any Pekelharings real or imaginary. On the other hand, the chemical technicalities of the deal weren't his responsibility either. 'No, you do it.'

John shuffled forward and Agatha, trying not to choke on his powerful odours, dragged herself half an inch deeper into the recess of her bed. John cringed at his own repulsive power and said in a voice pitched low to soften the offence, 'What does it mean to you, Agatha? *Eau prime*?'

Seeing no response in the girl, and capricious in his freedom from ÓDouwe's scrutiny, Gerrit attempted clarification. 'Dissolving silver in *eau prime*.'

John tutted at him and added, 'So that the silver tarnishes at an accelerated rate.'

Gerrit was not to be outdone. 'Using salts of ammonia – or indeed urine – to dissolve the silver and act as a fixative.'

Agatha's eyes had been closing. She forced them open and spoke through pale lips. 'Nothing, sir.' She looked from one to the other. 'I'm afraid I don't know very much about natural philosophy.'

John pushed forward. 'Really? You seem to know that much.'

Agatha tried not to inhale. 'Well, Miss Craebeckx said…'

Judith came forward. 'Let her rest, for God's sake.'

In the lull, Agatha made an effort to address ÓDouwe. 'Sir, is Madam my Mother alright?'

'What? Yes, she's alright…'

'May I see her?'

It was no good him reeling off a stream of half-baked answers that would need immediate modification after every likely objection: Mrs van Bosvelt was being cared for; she was being protected from herself;

she was being ministered to by the finest medics; she was in retreat from the strains of her life, attended by holy advisers. That sort of thing would do for now, though it could not put off forever the question of a personal visit.

He found that he had thrown aside the curtain and forced his way under Agatha's canopy and was trying to demonstrate the truth of what he was saying with the sheer weight of his presence.

Her face shimmered with miserable beauty. The translucent skin revealed tides of pink blood coursing hither and thither under the influence of grief. With his own face very close, she was a blur magnified by distress. He breathed towards it, wanting to soothe, but there was little in him but gall. 'Coming back from the dead. Is that something else only the rich do?' '

'Leave her be,' said Judith.

ÓDouwe stared but seemed not to see Judith's face. 'The Resurrection. There's a thing. And then, as you say, there is the simple light of day that falls on the world.' He searched Gerrit's and John's faces too for approval of this observation, scientific in its own way.

'Come on,' said Judith.

He gripped the arm that reached for him. 'God has His realm, we have ours. Isn't that it?'

Judith judged the need for reply. 'It's all God's. The separations are false.' She said it as if to a bright child who has drained patience with one question too many, equally astute and obtuse.

ÓDouwe let her lead him away from the bed, placing himself in her power for several paces, but he would not be ushered out of the room entirely.

Judith left him hovering at the margin, entered the bed herself, drew out the sobbing girl and held her in her arms. By chance – or Judith's sly arrangement – Agatha had her heaving back to ÓDouwe while Judith was able to gaze at him flatly beyond the girl's shoulder. But he was used to such hardships. He made the most of this one by appreciating the startling aesthetic harmony of the scene.

○

In such a creature, suspicion is easily aroused. Someone comes to the door asking for him, some scraggy weasel, whispering nasally into his ear, his breath filtered through green teeth, promising bad news, surely.

The whisperer, identifying himself as Hooft, blocked at the halfway mark of the stairs by ÓDouwe, said he had some information to impart. This was new. Informers usually sent letters, deliberately misspelled, handwriting all awry. The face under the dripping hat was all awry, all misspelled: nose wrong, eyes wrong, teeth very wrong. ÓDouwe (forearm concealing the blade of his knife) nearly said, 'What are you?' instead of 'Who are you?' But after that, he had his own information to impart, which was that he was not going to speak again until he was good and ready. He communicated this by holding his breath and not blinking.

'I mean, I mean. I mean about Mrs van Bosvelt,' said Hooft. 'Her brother-in-law. Your Honour's superior is meeting with him right now.'

ÓDouwe flexed his fingers on the knife-handle.

'He knows about the other girl.'

ÓDouwe showed the knife.

Hooft put his hands out in front of him. 'That's what I was told. I was told to say those words to you: Mr David van Bosvelt knows about the other girl.'

The knife rose.

'I don't know who it was. I've never seen him before.'

The point of the knife reached the informant's cheek.

'A short man, middle years, poor.' Hooft paused. 'Stank of drink.'

The knife-point rested on the cheek.

'He was just a messenger, like me. He said it the way I'm saying it, like he'd learned it.'

The knife-point turned into the cheek, drawing a trickle of blood.

'I'll take you to where I met him, but I've never seen him before.' The blade withdrew and Hooft made to slink away.

'Wait.'

Hooft stopped, did something – a shuffle on the spot – which caught ÓDouwe's attention for a second. Why send a man to send a man – possibly to send another man, and yet another? A string of them, each to be traced to a predecessor, and thence to an original messenger. An angel? Or a glittering devil waiting to deliver some ultimatum, some hot coal of a message… Or more likely the tracks were thoroughly swept and even the man before this one had gone back where he came from, or was already dead.

'He's there now?' said ÓDouwe. 'At the Superintendent Bailiff's office?' And then the question of what to do with the weasel: 'Go and report to my office.' ÓDouwe gave him an address. 'If you don't, I'll find you. If you do, there's gold.'

Hooft was intrigued by this offer and tilted his head to listen carefully to any of its fugitive ripples of meaning.

ÓDouwe listened with him, and (above the rain) heard the roar of folly. He called to Maria and sent her to fetch Backer and Meer who would serve as extra protection for Agatha. 'Now we'll wait.' And while they did so, ÓDouwe sat opposite Hooft whom he ordered to stand to attention, and beamed at him a rare perspicacity, unrelated to ordinary, outmoded, ways of judging persons. How long was it by the gently sibilant clock that ÓDouwe regarded this canal-rag of a man, who was all the while concentrating on looking stupid, bored, harmless, and who consequently found it very difficult to keep still? He shifted on his feet and twitched, and scratched his arm and his nose, and adjusted his hat, and looked at his boots and the floor and the ornaments on their various surfaces and the bottle (itself restless) at ÓDouwe's elbow, and wondered how the next phase of his mission (to kill this elusive policeman) could proceed.

Eventually, the fragments settled into a satisfactory pattern for ÓDouwe (the outcome of his calculations possibly including some reckless element of sacrifice and liberation). 'Alright, let's go,' he said.

○

David Davidsz. van Bosvelt, hearing of his sister-in-law's arrest, had presented himself at the door of the Superintendent Bailiff, Willem Jacobsz. Flinck, to make known his concern. That illustrious official, however, had washed his hands of all matters van Bosvelt and told him the whole thing was in his Assistant ÓDouwe's hands. Coming away from that interview, Mr van Bosvelt persuaded himself that he had been authorised to negotiate the terms of his sister-in-law's release with Mr ÓDouwe. When that very man presented himself in the street, Mr van Bosvelt was too surprised at the coincidence to speak, feeling himself vertiginously swept up in dreamlike manifestations, so that ÓDouwe (only provisionally recognising him from one of Mrs van Bosvelt's pictures) turned to Hooft for confirmation, blinking the rain out of his eyelashes. 'This is him? You're sure?'

Then the complicated business of uncrossing their purposes, Mr van Bosvelt's being the release from custody of his sister-in-law, Agatha's mother, and ÓDouwe's being the discovery of the truth about Agatha's missing twin. And this went on for some time with Hooft looking from one to the other, and roundabout for his accomplices.

Finally, ÓDouwe hustled an alarmed Mr van Bosvelt in the opposite direction from the Superintendent's house while explaining the reality of the situation to him: 'I could hang your sister-in-law tomorrow from her own eaves in broad daylight in front of a paying audience and receive a commendation from the High Sheriff. She is renowned as an insane blasphemer and she had murder on her mind and she very nearly succeeded in it. You want me to call a coven of predikants to argue the toss with you?'

Hooft peered into the rain-soaked shadows for his fellow assassins, thought of acting quickly on his own…

ÓDouwe stopped short, peered through the rain too. 'You see that man over there?'

'Who? Which one?' said Mr van Bosvelt.

'Him.' But there was no-one. 'Well, ten Brink's business is discretion also. He does his duty so well that even I can't keep track of him. Let's get in out of this.'

Inside the house under the ominous sign of The Plentiful Host, the noise was a hot substance rumbling within the heart of a thick band of smoke that began at knee level and became denser the higher it got. Within its tides, animated gargoyles pitched and yawed. It was as if these impressions alone were sufficient to make Uncle van Bosvelt drunk. Reluctantly he went before the policeman deep into this den, with Hooft following on behind, trying to see his friends among the gargoyles.

Was there a plan? Apart from letting a gloopy syrup of words and booze, booze and words seep into the atmosphere, slowing Uncle van Bosvelt down, slowing the whole room down, and working its way into everything?

Inevitably, the waterlogged bank gave way.

'People generally get the right idea about me, but you didn't. And you kept on not having any idea. You kept it up for quite a long time. But in the end, in the end…'

‘Where are we?’ Mr van Bosvelt was staring at his seventh drink.

‘Look at my eyes, my general countenance. They are those of a man busily formulating a new idea. Agatha got lost, yes. But found…?’

‘What’s happening?’

‘You and I are in a quite similar position on account of our invaluable services to the States. Without us, there’d be no States. We both benefit from a certain level of indulgence without which nothing could be accomplished. For instance, I’ve hanged the wrong man a few times, but in this case it’s too late for random acts of justice…’

‘Who are you again?’

ÓDouwe stared into the depths of his cup. Was it possible it was already empty? What did it mean that a cup could be empty? He filled it. ‘Feeling a bit out of date, like everything’s lagging behind. This is last week’s drink, for example, judging by the emotions that seem to be going along with it.’

‘Haven’t we been through all this already?’

‘A vision, perhaps feverishly produced in the mind only. An error was made. You and your brother, of necessity, out of family feeling, maintain a correspondence. When Agatha and her sister, her twin…’

‘I’m wondering…’

ÓDouwe raised a hand. Through a gap in the internal architecture, a man was staring at him. Certainly it was not ten Brink, but it could be one of his agents. ÓDouwe tilted his head to indicate curiosity, idling for now, but apt to sharpen. The man tilted his own head in brazen imitation. ÓDouwe looked away, embarrassed, then slyly looked back. Still he was being watched from under the thick brim of the hat – a hat dented in the same style as his own. He squinted and the man squinted back. He scratched his nose, and the man copied him. It was as if a spirit, by an internal impulse, were creating a double of itself. Then he saw it was merely a mirror. He was being haunted by his own reflection, but how unfamiliar it had seemed, how transformed by nothing more substantial than belief that it was other than itself. What's true of your own face might well be true – truer – of many other things. 'You think you know about your family,' he went on, 'but what do you know? Only what you've been told or shown. I'm only talking about a simple deception. Even before we start to think about the reason for it… You see, I won't go so far as to even whisper that you are the real Father of those girls. That would be purely a random guess based on no more evidence than a woman divided against herself, a hidden daughter, a substituted corpse, and a man suddenly attentive to the family now that the obstacle is removed. Grief would explain it, yes, but it doesn't supply details…'

'Now look here!'

ÓDouwe drank from his cup, but was wary of draining it to the bottom remembering what had happened before. 'The husband of the lady in question, your brother, whom I've never met. Look, first he makes his public, his professional errors. Then he leaves his wife. Takes the other twin, or one of them, whichever one. One of them dies, is killed by some hand unknown, or by someone closer to home. Then there's the substitution. The one that was killed, that was the one left with her Mother. So now she is replaced by the one that was taken away all those years ago when they were very small. There is no flicker of recognition when I tell the surviving twin about this. That's when the Father had his trouble and abandoned them. So he's full of remorse. A revenge of some kind against the Mother. He's somewhere nearby all the time. Agnes's and Agatha's Father. What? Oh, it's just a name I made up for her since no-one will tell me. Anyway, he takes the daughter he's lived with for fifteen years, gives her to the Mother as a replacement, a gift, to stop her from making more trouble for him. It's the kind of mess you make when you've committed a terrible act on the spur of the moment, and afterwards you want to do everything you can to erase it. So yes:

how is the new twin going to play the part of the first twin, of Agatha, so convincingly? She is in thrall to her Father…'

'None of this can really matter all that much, surely…'

'Drink more. One more. Just one more. One more…'

'What?'

'It's all about the transition, about leaving the tavern, knowing the previous eight hours were leading up to it.'

'I suppose…'

'Is that it, though, eh? Your fate is sealed, is that it? Ah, but destiny is such an intricate thing, and bad religion is no substitute for good religion, don't you think? And that idiot, what's his name? John's friend – do you know John Norvell? English boy, crippled arm, educated – Deyckardt? Was that his name? Thinking God can't be deceiving him. That's what we have for a philosopher?'

'I forget. Are we on a boat?'

'Most important of all is to obliterate getting up in the morning and going to bed at night and preparing to eat and keeping appointments and remembering to say the same kinds of things to different kinds of people…'

'No (I think).'

'This is her opportunity to be reunited with her Mother whom she hasn't seen since she was a baby. Well, she doesn't remember her, but children, mothers, who knows? Powerful feelings, beyond reason. This is the condition he sets for her joining her Mother. The secrecy, the lie. But yes, still, yes, I know: once she's there, she could let the cat out of the bag. She could tell her Mother. She could tell me. But she can't because the Father has already murdered her sister. That's the power he has over her. She's terrified. He has told her all about Agatha, how she talks, what she does. He's told her to feign loss of memory to cover over the differences…'

'A twin?' Uncle van Bosvelt peered into the dregs.

'Look at the evidence.'

'But what evidence?'

'This!' ÓDouwe spread his arms out to encompass the whole of the present situation, venue, props and all. He saw two of the gargoyles separating from the band of smoke.

'Yes, but what exactly?'

'Everything!' said ÓDouwe, blinking the sweat out of his eyes. 'Everything!' He paused to consider his companions.

Hooft was swaying gently above his own cup, waiting, waiting, his concealed knife – the one he had not handed in at the door – pressing into his thigh.

The data were spinning, reconfiguring, settling. ÓDouwe put his face close to Mr van Bosvelt's, showed the teeth, the yellow eyeballs. 'I don't know why you did it,' he whispered.

○

Ten Brink was beckoning the musicians. The noise of the many boots in the passageway had already interrupted their tune, and obedient to that powerful finger, they filed out silently.

And now it beckoned Judith. She was alarmed, knowing something of ÓDouwe's mutterings against ten Brink. She would not go to him. Something bad was happening. She moved closer to Agatha.

'I just want to talk to you. I won't enter without your consent.'

'Then leave the house.'

'I have the Assistant Superintendent Bailiff's permission to go this far. I need yours to go further.' His body was urging itself forward, but he kept the soles of his heavy boots on his side of the threshold. Lennep's thin face could be glimpsed over his shoulder.

'Where is he? I'll speak to him first,' said Judith. 'His men are coming any minute. Maria's bringing them.'

'Calmly, calmly.' Ten Brink's boots crossed the threshold. 'He is no longer in charge. You know…' He shrugged.

Laughably – ten Brink did laugh – Judith tried to block Agatha's body with her own. He reached out slowly for her arm, as if it were a poisonous snake. Oopjen stood fascinated by these motions. Judith surprised him by running behind Agatha.

'No, no, no. You don't seem to understand.' He beckoned Lennep and waved a hand at Agatha. Lennep wiped his mouth as he approached.

'Stop!' Judith boomed at him and he stopped. She then cursed ten Brink and threw a glass at him but it travelled wide of his head. Still she wouldn't fully surrender so that he had to go to her (at nominal cost) and complete the motion of his glove on her arm.

'You know your friend van Oelst is not well. You should visit him.' He passed her to Lennep, but she would not let him touch her. The three of them left the room. There were more men in the passage ready to escort her away. She looked in vain for the faces of Backer and Meer among them.

Ten Brink pulled the door to and stood guard. After a few moments, it squeaked open again. 'Get back in!' he yelled at the eye hovering in the crack, and the door slammed shut.

Harmen Flinck, parcel in hand, adjusted the scarf over his nose and kept his head down, but Judith spotted him in the shadows anyway and watched his lanky form appear and disappear between the torsos of her captors. As she was handed into a waiting barge, he moved towards the van Bosvelt house and she called out to him, but he didn't hear her or pretended not to.

Lennep idled after Flinck towards his guardpost and almost collided with his back as Flinck stopped short under the sign of The Lions Triumphant and began to study the front door through slitted eyes. Rather than stepping through it, Flinck, on the verge of success, was wishing to use his supreme powers to melt it out of existence with fiery beams. And indeed in a gilded cavern of his mind, he did see the paint blister and crack, the wood scorch and flare, and Agatha, object of his long quest, revealed just the other side of it framed by a spreading ring of flame. Lennep weighed the bag of money at his belt while staring at the side of Flinck's face wondering what he was waiting for. The jingling coins distracted Flinck out of his trance.

Inside, Flinck delivered his parcel into Agatha's trembling hand. 'Judith is quite safe, but she must be persuaded. I'm here to save you. You are quite safe.'

Agatha looked past him to the blurry silhouettes of ten Brink's heels showing at the gap under the door. 'Where's Mr ÓDouwe?'

'He has been removed from your case. Mr ten Brink is the new man. Judith won't be harmed. You'll see her again, and soon. There's no rush. We must have something to calm ourselves. Some wine – or beer will do. Here, take this.'

Had Agatha expected this visit? Had there been premonitions, swooping augurs? Hers was a mind fertilised by tedium, repetition, captivity. She was calm. Intimations borne of a vigorous new strain of perspicacity, augmented by the occasionally whispered name of Flinck out of ÓDouwe's hearing. And certainly Flinck had been prowling the edge of the policeman's territory, gaining the confidence of the servants, selecting the weakest link (Lennep) in the chain.

Agatha was imagining entertainment, intrigue. She pulled out of the parcel a large ring of the type betrothed couples give each other. It bore a circular design showing in tiny detail a faun embracing – chastely, she ascertained – a nymph. She took the undiluted beer he offered her and drank.

Oopjen meanwhile flitted this way and that so that Flinck had to tell her to be still, and when she was, he handed her a loaded purse, ballast for her skittering emotions. This set her off on another journey, even more intricately conceived and purely of the mind, towards a revision of her part in this rendezvous. She was of that breed of creature blindly loyal to whichever brute rules the troupe until his power wanes and he is superseded by a rival.

Flinck returned to Agatha. 'I wish only to give you a gift. Make of it what you will. Nothing is certain in these days. Who knows what the future holds?' He refilled her glass and held it out to her. 'Don't place it on your finger, whatever you do. Put it in your pocket, or hide it away somewhere.' Agatha took the glass, and he waited until she drank before resuming. 'Think of it as a symbolic token of some replacement of emotion, some new arrangement to offset the passing of the old.' He stooped to transfer the heat of his hands to hers. 'Isn't it nearly your birthday, after all?'

'No.'

'But recently?' He let go of her and made a serious face. 'Here you are in this house, a girl not yet of age, at the centre of the most complicated legal wranglings imaginable. But you aren't a prisoner. Within the Law, the *Law*, you're free. And one might add that you have certain responsibilities – to do with your rank, I mean.'

'Like what?' Agatha pouted, wary but sensitive to an airborne tang of freedom.

'To enjoy yourself. To show that you're enjoying yourself. Beyond this.' His outstretched hand almost grazed the painting on its easel by the window. He went closer to study it.

'Painting is redemption. Miss Craebeckx says so.'

Flinck was startled. 'And you will have many opportunities in the future to hear her words of wisdom.'

'And Socrates in old age writing poems to obey his spirit's demand to make art. He'd always said philosophy was the highest art, but at the end, just in case… I'd like to read them, but they're nowhere to be found. Judith says it's a yet higher art, this "nowhere to be found."'

Flinck replenished Agatha's empty glass of beer. 'You shall see her soon. And you shall have all necessary means to pursue this art of yours. I know all the important men.' He wagged his finger at the picture again. 'That is a very well painted flower.'

'More and more like the thing. And in the case of the living thing, more and more a breaking of God's stipulation not to.'

○

ÓDouwe raged around Agatha's chamber cursing inventively – a little too inventively, as if he were enjoying his fury, relishing and refining it. Was he relieved after all? Certainly the burden was lessened knowing that Judith was innocent of any crime.

Dark blood (his own) oozed through the thick bandage on his hand. There was more blood (that of Hooft, Hooft's accomplices, possibly even Uncle van Bosvelt's) on his coat, his face, his hat.

Everyone's surreptitious glances goaded him further and he thrashed at them with his glove – a humiliation he had previously only inflicted on Lennep. Maria and Oopjen cringed under those slaps. Meer caught most of Backer's share as well as his own, though Backer suffered the extra insult of having his precious liripipe grabbed from his head, thrown to the ground and stamped on. Lennep managed by some miracle of oversight to stay out of the windmill's range. All shuffled back towards the walls. When their master drew his sword, Backer felt he should put his hand upon his own, but ÓDouwe only swung the weapon above his head a few times before hacking at the ornaments, the curtains, the furniture, saving for last the drapery around the girl's bed on which he finally spent his marvellous wrath. Then he rested. 'You've been fucking the maids, you useless cunts, instead of doing your jobs.'

Maria and Oopjen blushed as they wailed.

'They wouldn't let us,' said Meer in a sincere tone of regret. Backer gave him a quick look to shut him up.

'Who saw her last? And make sure you tell me the truth or it's the punish-room for the lot of you.'

Backer instantly decided that if he were sure that was to be their fate, then his master would not leave this room alive.

But ÓDouwe saw it was useless. Agatha was long gone. Now he was struck dumb, gazing into the middle-distance, seeming unable to imagine her anywhere but in this room. He poured himself a generous measure to quench his thirst. 'All shall be punished,' he said breathily as the wine-fumes wheezed in his throat. 'All.' He surveyed the faces, noted the alarm and shame they bore. 'And where the hell were you two?'

Meer made no sign of preparing to reply. Backer delivered for both of them his well-rehearsed answer: 'We were drinking with the Watch, sir. We had no way of knowing what was going on here.'

Maria quivered as ÓDouwe turned to her. 'I'm so very sorry, sir. I didn't think to… I couldn't find them…' She started weeping again.

ÓDouwe sifted through the guts of Backer and Meer's tale in search of its flaw, its obvious flaw… But first Lennep – whose (latest) bribe still rattled in his belt; whose stupidity took as its highest form disloyalty; whose fate was accelerating towards him.

To Lennep, it had been an omen, as sure as a one-eyed witch's murmur, his being spared that glove. He knew this, while telling himself it wasn't so: relief and dread mingled unnaturally. But his fate was now shaping itself: for each blow from Backer or Meer, a groan. For each cut, a ringing howl, but no news of the absconder, only the names of ten Brink and of Flinck, over and over again. And those names alone no matter the blow, the cut, the twist, the stab. Maria and Oopjen were required to stay. They howled too, and retched upon the boards, and trembled, and pissed themselves, and keened in primal chorus at the molten horror of the world as their sins found them out, so that Oopjen told how she was assured by ten Brink that all was legal. Then she fainted and Maria hurled herself on top of her, shrieking into the folds of her skirt.

Lennep had nothing more to say and little means to say it. Backer and Meer bent sweating and panting over the blood-soaked heap.

'Stand aside,' said ÓDouwe, holding his sword high in his own bloody hand.

Afterwards, he surveyed the destruction as if it were the result of some freak natural catastrophe – an icy tornado, or a convulsion from the boiling deep. Lennep's head, bearing no resemblance to its former state, lay at ÓDouwe's feet. No longer heeding his audience, ÓDouwe considered the head for a long while before quitting the desecrated chamber, dragging his sword after him.

He wandered through the corridors fondly reminiscing on the life that had once teemed in that house. His doleful trail took him to the grand salon where he slumped into a chair and helped himself to wine and a pipe. The van Bosvelt portraits stared back at him. There in the middle around that fat foreign fireplace were the half dozen versions of the mysterious child, painted at various stages in her life. The mysterious and absent child. Or three of one child and three of another. He got up and moved in closer: a yellow-haired baby, a flush-cheeked toddler, a sprouting girl. Six in all, but not all by the same hand. The three on the left were coarser, browner. The three on the right finer, pinker and a bit smaller. Two painters for two children. But they usually paint the children together, don't they? Well, only in the abodes of the sane, which this is not.

'What's in a glass of wine besides wine?'

One thirty-second of an inch out, an edge of a paper protruded from behind one of the paintings depicting the girl at her youngest. He held his pipe in his teeth and teased the paper free between his knife-point and a blood-stained fingernail. Had these been turned to face the wall according to custom when there is a death, they would have been perfectly visible all along. The secreted item was a small silk-covered placard trimmed with cream lace, a white square pinned to its centre. This treasure was the palpable record of the birth of a child. The white square denoted a girl. If there were another such object, it would show the existence of a sister. If the placards were identical in age that would suggest twins.

He lifted the companion portrait to this one from the wall and flipped it over, and there it was, the other placard. He called the maids to him excitedly.

They came running. 'She's nowhere to be found, sir,' they wailed. 'We looked in the trees.'

'Recognise these?' He was euphoric, flushed, wild-eyed, sober. He held the items up, smeared with his bloody fingerprints.

'They're birth cards, sir,' said Maria, not comprehending the joy.

'For?'

They approached to inspect the items. 'For a girl. Are they Agatha's?'

ÓDouwe put the two placards on a table next to each other, kept adjusting them with his fingers until they were exactly parallel. His eyes were shining, perhaps with tears. 'See?' he said, 'You see? They're the same.' He tilted his head back and issued two curling streams of tobacco smoke from his nose.

‘Are they?’ said Maria hesitantly.

‘What?’

‘Exactly the same?’

‘Doesn’t matter. There’s a sister. We have the proof. They’re close enough, look at them, to be, for them to be twins, the two girls, the sisters, twins.’

‘Sir.’ Maria could barely dare to make herself heard. ‘I don’t think they’re exactly—’

‘Close enough for me.’

‘The lace on this one is not as good. The paper is thinner,’ she said.

Oopjen stood behind her noting these obvious facts in terrorised silence.

‘So what?’ said ÓDouwe.

‘They always have two, the rich ones, both for the same child. One for Sunday best, one for weekdays,’ Maria explained slowly.

‘Two?’ ÓDouwe went on, oblivious to the effect he was spreading. ‘And here they are. Two.’ He poured himself a triumphant glassful.

○

It was a dance performed backwards. The whore Aeltje was Flinck’s mirror in which nothing of himself was reflected. Were they deliberately confusing Agatha with their wiles? What is like pleasure, but not the thing itself? Flinck, unseen by the blindfolded musicians (who wearily continued their work), raised his hand in an artificial gesture of the romantic orator, and staring directly at Agatha, gave voice to the matters on his mind. But all she could make out of his recitation was its quotient of honey.

All of their charades reached Agatha through the bubbles in her drink, and she was mesmerised by the gentle arising thereof out of seeming nothing.

Now Aeltje was an animal and Mr Flinck was appreciating her. Where did that leave Agatha? Here, not there. She edged towards them stiffnecked as if bearing a heavy crown on her head and tilted her large eyes in their direction.

'There's something different about you,' Flinck said, fluttering his fingers at her. 'What can it be?'

Agatha looked down at herself and vaguely wondered what had become of her clothes. She was relieved to see she was not entirely naked though: Harmen's ring was still on her finger.

Aeltje at all times did nothing but her job. In this instance, she was discreetly supplying allure where Mr Flinck's charm flagged.

'Did Judith ever entertain you as we are doing?' Mr Flinck enquired of Agatha, as if civilised conversation were not out of place under these circumstances.

One face took the place of another, and then another, and then back again.

On waking, Agatha tried to penetrate through the baked crackling, the dancing blood patterns and the mist behind her eyes that glittered with flashing points of pain. Her nakedness struck her like the impact from a fall. Her skin seemed feverish, mottled and gaudy. Her fellow damned still shared her pit, but were oblivious to its torments. They were all tangled together, a many-limbed example of an unspeakable error.

She tried to detach herself. Flinck stirred, smiled and gripped her tighter. Aeltje woke too, stretched, yawned loudly and coughed. Her nakedness by contrast to Agatha's lacked shame or guile. It seemed to lack nakedness even, like a child's body, merely an extension, a container. Mr Flinck's nakedness had no meaning of its own, partaking of the values of other bodies. Agatha spun away in alarm from the obscene realism of what he had euphemised as his *soldat de l'avant garde,* which was pointing directly at her. He laughed gently.

What abominations had she consented to? Panicked by shame, she freed herself, sprang out of the bed and scrambled for her clothes. Flinck propped himself up on an elbow, and with a carefully calibrated hint of the pathetic, said, 'Don't go.' In her haste, she became tangled, and endured the pleasure he took in her disadvantage. He tried again. 'Where will you go?' The full moon of his face hung somewhere east of her ear, visible as a blur pocked with black craters for eyes and mouth.

'Home,' she said in a voice that crept out of her.

'How can you now?'

Aeltje had sat up in the bed. Daylight revealed the stresses of repetitive usage in the fabric of her body. The ends of her knotted hair hung over her sagging, blue-veined breasts. Belly-folds settled over pale marker-lines. The curdled blood under the skin bypassed ancient traces of violence.

Whatever happened, Agatha could not return to her prison. There was too much madness, repression, secrecy, silence, lies – and lechery from those stable animals hired to guard her. And now, she was informed by Flinck, ÓDouwe was hunting her. The feather-tipped wings of his fury were already brushing the air around her. His animals had visited Mrs Bleckker, and since Agatha was not there but elsewhere, Madam had sent them away empty-handed. But the power of Mr Flinck's money could penetrate only so far and for so long. There was nowhere for her to go. It would be impossible to remain at Judith's apartment undetected. For the present, she was at the mercy of her defiler. She threw the cap down that she was trying to untwist, dropped to her knees and cried.

'There, there,' cooed Flinck pulling on a dressing gown and waving Aeltje away. The moth rolled out of the bed and went off, still naked, slapping her soles on the boards. 'You're safe now,' Flinck went on. 'Mr

ÓDouwe is not the force you all think he is. My Father is, after all, his employer.' He touched the tears streaking down her cheeks.

She twisted away and wiped them herself.

'Did we not have fun, after all?' he said.

She dredged from the well of her chest a profound note of disgust and took refuge in the slick membrane forming between her face and her palms.

○

'Fucking foreigners.'

La, la, la. Newly appointed Assistant Superintendent Bailiff Roel ten Brink polished the lens of his telescope and aimed it at the sky. The moon is a rocky ball. So much for the heavens. Oh look, down there, that's funny: a pigeon with a ring of bread around its neck. It must have pecked its way through the middle and then—. Fanned out for his inspection, the whole of the region between the megaliths in the northeast and the line of gibbets stretching out to the south.

In his favourite chair imported to the high tower on the City wall, his legs swinging under the table, a cup of weak beer at his elbow, he dipped bread into his stew. At his other elbow lay some kind of a complicated device full of coins surrounded by springs and cogs, with a spoiled scroll of paper attached. Open next to the steaming bowl was one of Norvell's comprehensive notebooks into which ten Brink occasionally added a note of his own in the margin.

What other innovations could be dreamt up to reverse the tide of sin? A device equivalent to the telescope that could magnify sound – but then all the town would hear the din… Or by the careful observation of lip movements to understand what everyone was saying: the old man and his slave hunched over their table lying to each other; the midget girl everyone's so keen on, nursing that big-eyed cat in her lap; that coven of painters ranged around their blasphemous totem; those bookworms comparing notes on gauges of canal or whatever it is they're up to; the clapped-out old whoremistress rolling her dead eye at the walls of her attic where she's been abandoned by her fat understudy.

Detail, detail, detail, rippling outward, repeating, modifying, diminishing. They think they're clawing their way to the top, whereas they're all upside down clawing their way to the bottom.

And ÓDouwe, sovereign example of this principle, disgraced, bandaged, blind drunk: a candle stuttering in front of that faded purple-grey rectangle he looted from the painters' darkroom, impatiently awaiting his own sombre fate, muttering hopelessly, 'Everything's the same, everything's the same.'

BEFORE

As in a recurring dream, Paul, on hearing a commotion, hunkered down out of sight. Between the trees, there was movement. He crept around a trunk and concealed himself behind its roots. A little way off was a small clearing into which walked a group of strangers: two boys and a girl. The girl, Agatha van Bosvelt, was dressed in a simple white shift and had a garland of Spring flowers in her hair, though it was not Spring. The boys were naked, horned, had hairy animal haunches and hooves instead of human legs and feet, and they were smiling. They seemed to Paul about his own age.

Moonlight played through the girl's thin garment revealing, now and then, her shape. She was older than the others.

Paul held himself still, controlled his breath in case its movement stirred the grass near his face and drew their attention.

The terror that should have come didn't: the young people in the clearing seemed so carefree, so happy and innocent, so harmless, so playful. But terror hovered at the edge of this gaiety and kept him concealed where he was.

They seemed to be dancing or playing some complicated game with their hands, intertwining their fingers, interweaving their hair, snaking their arms around each other in tangled patterns that he could not follow. Between their hairy haunches, the fauns' members seemed to play dancing games of their own.

One of them lifted the girl's wreath of flowers from her head while the other raised her shift and slipped it from her.

The dance continued around her. For a moment, she tried to cover herself modestly, before throwing up her hands and laughing for joy. She was cream-coloured in the moonlight. A pale orange halo outlined her hair which seemed to never lie still. Some breeze that Paul could not feel played heedlessly with it.

Giggling, the fauns turned the girl this way and that admiring her naked body. They kissed her ears, stroked her shoulders, her hair, her limbs, her fingers and her toes. She giggled too at these naughty little familiarities. And she stroked the boys in turn: their horns, their always smiling faces, the luxurious pelts on their thighs…

One of the fauns weighed the round apple of her breast and tweaked a pink nipple. The other caressed the hair below her belly with a long fingernail.

Their voices were like the rustling of the leaves high in the trees where the stars are – mixed with the faraway calls of the night creatures. In response to the fauns' instructions, the girl picked up her garland of flowers and her white shift. By some careless wave of a hairy hand a bonfire sprang to life and the girl threw the garland and the shift onto it where they smouldered and were consumed.

Keeping close to her, one in front, one behind, they murmured in her ear. One reached up to her face and closed one of her eyes while holding the other open. She seemed to understand these strange movements and kept her eyes that way. The other faun guided her hands to her head and continued his murmuring. To Paul's unaccustomed ear, that alien voice reached him in the guise of a spring bubbling through a fissure. The girl obliged and reached up and pulled her own head from her shoulders. She lifted it higher and higher until all the tendons and skin tore asunder with small snapping sounds and she placed the head carefully on the ground at her feet. The open eye swivelled uncertainly in its socket. Dark streams of blood coursed down from the wound over her breasts. The fauns clapped and gambolled gleefully and helped her to lie down in the moss next to her head. They stood over her then, adjusting her limbs and admiring their work.

The blazing fire reduced to an orange glow.

Those playful fauns, before they tripped away arm in arm, turned to Paul and gave him a friendly wave and seemed to say his name, though it could just as easily have been the sound of the moon's gravity pulling at the vegetation of the forest. The terror rushed in on him then and he recoiled behind the trunk of his tree and shut his eyes. When he dared to peek out again, they were gone, the fire was nearly extinguished and the girl lay still on the ground.

He crept out from his hiding place and crawled towards her on all fours. Her blood was oozing into the soil. The open eye was immobile in its socket and there was no more life in the body. He picked up her head. It was surprisingly heavy. He nearly dropped it. Whimpering, he tried to fix it back into place on her shoulders. Her blood smeared over his hands and clothes.

He gave up on the idea and sat next to her, overwhelmed by sorrow.

In the background to this miserable scene, in the city on the plain, the Virgin City, the impenetrable cloud of smoke issuing from the fires, the lamps and the hundred thousand tobacco pipes signalled the successful inauguration of a new kermis.

These delicate preparations completed, the girl, still naked, still besmirched by her own red blood, with her head tucked under her arm, one of its eyes open, one closed, took her proper place in the procession.

Suddenly, from far off and high up, a commanding voice bellowed, 'A great soul has fallen!' and the murmuring crowd fell silent.

She strained to see above this multitude and found she could improve her view if she held her head high in the air above herself. This gave her an advantage over most of the others, and she didn't care how silly she might look.

She saw that she was at the lowest level among the groundlings who made up the majority of the spectators. There were thousands of them, a sea of heads – mostly still attached to their shoulders – all turned in the same direction.

At the centre of all this attention was a magnificent bier in the form of an enormous rough-hewn rock the size of a ship, being drawn along at stately pace by a vast host of white mares – thirty or so abreast, sinuous and gorgeous as nakedness itself. Neither rock nor horses touched the ground. Rather, they floated a foot or two above it, disturbing no grain of it, though the rumbling din of the hooves and the shearing groan of the rock were plain to hear. And though the horses maintained a tightly disciplined formation, there was no drover behind them and no sign of any harness, so that if they wore any, they were made of such fine stuff as to be as invisible as the thin air itself.

Meanwhile, cowering behind the roots of his tree, apparent to any in this throng that cared to look, but himself blind to them, was the scrawny, forlorn figure of the living vagrant boy with blood on his hands. His large eyes, glistening in a faraway moonlight – curiously, since everything else was unfolding in the full light of the sun – seemed fixed on some other spectre, a horror from another time, perhaps brought forward according to some mystic purpose, to run concurrently with the present ceremonial.

On it went, this imposing funerary vision until the rock slid past where the girl was standing. She stood on tip-toes and stretched her arms up even higher to get a better view. On top of the rock there lay outstretched the form of a creature not unlike the fauns she had encountered earlier in the wood, but much older and hairier. Flowers of every kind, and of every season, all in full bloom, were heaped about this important corpse, and they sent out in all directions their ravishing confusion of perfumes.

At the front of the bustling groundlings lining all the route, innumerable nymphs wept bitterly as their hero glided past on his rock, and in their anguish they rent their flimsy garments exposing areas of milky flesh.

When the rock had passed on, the girl turned to a youth of her own age who stood next to her. 'Who is he?' she asked. The youth, naked like herself, his face as beautiful as a mirror, stared at her in surprise without answering. She tilted her head to look him up and down, her eye lingering curiously on his uncovered sex, until she was diverted by the strange marks on his limbs – deep bloody gashes that seemed newly made.

'Why do you carry your head like that?' he asked her, but before she could respond, an usher loomed at them and sternly told them to be silent, face the front and do their duty.

The grand bier was now approaching the tiers of important personages ranged under their colonnade. Some were gods of impressive rank, though the higher gods were notably absent. Each of those higher gods was however represented by some diminutive aspect or lower-echelon agent, as the case may be.

There was the blood-drenched Xiuhtecuhtl, Sul carrying about her the heady scent of her sulphurous spring, Un-nefer the beautiful hare, Hades under his helmet of darkness, Agni with his dreamy Soma plant, and not forgetting Nergal attended by his butler Bibbu. There were many more besides, too many to name, but each one of them would be revealed by expert inspection to be a deity either of fire or of the netherworld. And the whole host of them was fleshed out with every manner of mini-godlet and angelic arbiter.

The humble avatar of an ascendant power, the being formerly known as Yeshua Ha-Notsri also attended, bearing the sacred marks of his apotheosis, holding himself aloof from these ceremonials, but doing sufficient duty as witness, and lingering just long enough to have his presence and his state recognised by those – mainly of the groundlings –

who might benefit from it.

The girl, having in the past seen many pictures of him, indeed recognised him as he leaned gracefully against the twisted trunk of an ancient olive tree. And before he faded forever into the undifferentiated luminosity of the background, she whispered the word 'Jesus' and experienced in her simple little heart a spreading warmth.

The great rock-bier, dragged forward by its thousands of obedient horses, came level with the high guests beneath their colonnade. Each in turn, and according to peculiar style, made acknowledgement of the fact and perhaps, here and there, some even made a gesture of regret or obeisance.

The present journey of this illustrious personage on this plane thus completed, the horses responding to some invisible signal or divine urge began to rise into the air, the first rank first, then the next, and so on, so that the whole legion of them snaked lithely up towards the ice-blue heavens towing behind them this paradoxical rock bearing its still and silent cargo, shedding all the while over the crowd of witnesses below, alive or dead, mortal or divine, its additional burden of many-coloured blossoms.

And the stentorian voice of the master of ceremonies was charged up again to deliver its final announcement: 'A kid, he is fallen into milk!'

As if taking this enigmatic statement as its cue, Shamash-Heru-Helios in all its blinding glory slipped out of the sky into the ocean, causing it to seethe and throw up gouts of steam.

After a pause, during which the steam wafted away and the waters cooled, there was a fresh disturbance on the sea's surface: a great swell followed by a white frothing turmoil announced the rising of Ashimbabbar-Men-Selene, smaller, paler and cooler than its predecessor, companion rather than rival to the stars, it settled comfortably in its place in the heavens.

Unswerving from its trajectory, the chariot of the dead god sped towards this renewed full moon and slipped behind it. This seemed to constitute the final moment of the funerary rite.

The groundlings began to stir and exchange looks and comments and then finally disperse.

The gods and their acolytes no longer occupying their colonnade had evidently returned to wherever they had come from, as had the colonnade itself.

(Likewise, the vagrant boy, along with his tree, the roots that had concealed him, and those other soft moonbeams which had illuminated him.)

Unsure what to do, the girl once again turned to the naked youth next to her, but he only glanced back briefly before shuffling away with the rest into the darkness which newly surrounded them on all sides, so she decided to head towards that same darkness herself.

From *A History of the Low Countries* by Jean-Jacques Fleurant, Paris 1716

The 'trouble' issuing from those religious and historical complications alluded to in my late friend John Norvell's notebooks (vol. II, page 159) concerns a rumour – quite unsubstantiated by any evidence whatsoever – of the death and subsequent resurrection of a fifteen-year-old girl of the family Van Bosvelt who were of the regent class.

That her corpse was supposedly discovered in the Biesbosch – or Bee Wood – on the outskirts of Dordrecht, for example, or that her return to life supposedly coincided with the first observed instance of the transit of the planet Venus across the face of the Sun, in themselves constitute no more than a web of felicitous if not downright poetic connections of no actual substance.

It altogether smacks of the legend of the patron Saint Sura of that City who, having worked on the building of the chapel whose site is now occupied by their famous church of Our Lady, was murdered by jealous colleagues in a dispute over money and subsequently returned from the grave – to the general consternation – entire, alive and in vengeful mood.

The whole pyre, in my opinion, was kindled and lit by a common creeping terror that the predicted events contained within the visions of Daniel and St. John the Divine were about to unfold within that particular generation, which, as can plainly be seen in this our reasonable age, has failed to be the case.

THE END

Key Principles in History

1 A Night Ape

2 After the Death of the Goat God

3 I, Igor

4 Silence

5 The Mansions of the Millions of Mansions